HALFWAY TO NOWHERE

STEENA HOLMES
ELENA AITKEN

This is a work of fiction. The events and characters described herein are imaginary and are not intended to refer to specific places or living persons. The opinions expressed in this manuscript are solely the opinions of the author and do not represent the opinions or thoughts of the publisher. The author has represented and warranted full ownership and/or legal right to publish all the materials in this book.

Halfway to Nowhere

All Rights Reserved

Copyright © 2013 Elena Aitken & Steena Holmes

Version 4.0

This book may not be reproduced, transmitted, or stored in whole or in part by any means, including graphic, electronic, or mechanical without the express written consent of the publisher except in the case of brief quotations embodied in critical articles and reviews. Your support of author rights is appreciated.

Sista' Books

DEAR READER

Steena and Elena here!

When we decided to join forces and write a story together from two different viewpoints, we thought it would be a lot of fun. And it was! It was also an incredibly interesting and emotional story line to explore. We are both thrilled with the result, and it's our sincerest hope that you fall in love with Nikki and Becky and their experience as much as we did.

We both love to connect with readers and chat about our love for books which means we'd love for you to sign up for our newsletters so we can stay in touch (plus we're both giving away copies of one of our own individual series...so you know you want to sign up!)

For Steena's newsletter click HERE!

For Elena's newsletter click HERE!

We can't wait to hear from you!

Steena & Elena

CHAPTER 1

~*Nikki*~

Nikki Landon hadn't been down the main street in Halfway, Montana for ten years, but it might as well have been yesterday for all the changes there were. She pulled up to a single flashing red light. That was new. *Okay, maybe some things did change.* She adjusted the rearview mirror and peeked into the back seat at her son, Ryan. *Definitely*, she thought as she stole a glance at his blond hair and sparkling blue eyes taking in everything outside his window. *Some things changed a whole lot.*

She tapped her brake pedal, but with no other cars in sight, Nikki eased her vehicle through the intersection and continued down the street.

"That's Grounds," she said to Ryan. She rapped on the glass, pointing to the coffee shop where she'd spent many hours, pretending to do homework.

"Do they have hot chocolate?"

"Of course." She smiled. "They also have the best macchiato

I've ever tasted. Maybe we can stop in and get one sometime?" Nikki bit her lip, regretting the words the second they left her mouth. She didn't plan to be in Halfway long enough to start visiting her old haunts. With any luck at all, she'd be able to deal with her mother's house and get out before anyone noticed. As if that would be possible in a town the size of Halfway.

Nikki tried not to dwell on all the reasons she didn't want to be there; the list would be way too long. She needed to stay focused, close up her mother's estate, and say goodbye to her past once and for all.

But first, food. She pulled her car into an open space on the street in front of the Evergreen Grocer and looked in the mirror again. "Will you be okay for a few minutes? I just need to grab us a few things for dinner because I'm not sure what Grandma had in the…" She drifted off when she saw Ryan's face crumple.

Nikki twisted around in her seat the best she could and grabbed her son's hand. "Hey, buddy. It's okay to be sad, you know?"

He nodded and sucked in his lips, trying to hold back the tears.

Nikki blinked hard. She refused to cry in front of Ryan. "Grandma was very special and I miss her too." She squeezed Ryan's hand. "And when we get to the house, I'll be able to show you the cool collection of spoons she had."

"Spoons?" He raised his eyebrow, clearly not believing her.

"It's true," she said. "Grandma collected spoons from all over. And you'll be able to see them, as soon as we get there." Nikki let go of his hand and patted his knee. "But first, we need food. How does frozen pizza sound?"

Ryan's eyes lit up the way she knew they would. "And fries?"

She shook her head, but said, "Okay. But you have to have milk with dinner."

"Deal."

Satisfied for the time being, Nikki left Ryan to play on his tablet and got out of the car. She froze for a minute before walking into the Evergreen. The problem with trying to sneak into a small town you'd run away from ten years earlier was that it was impossible. Everyone knew everyone and everyone's business. She had as much chance of sneaking into town undetected as a kitten cuddling up in a wolf den. Not that she was some helpless kitten. No, Nikki could hold her own. And besides, there were only two people she needed to avoid.

The bells jingled overhead as she pushed her way into the store and Nikki cringed. She scanned the space, but no one was looking her way. Yet. Needing to hurry, she grabbed a wire basket from the rack by the door and moved down the first aisle. She was counting on the fact that the Wilsons still owned the store and hadn't changed the layout, and from what she could tell, it was exactly the same.

Nikki located the frozen food section and tossed in a pepperoni pizza, a bag of fries and at the last minute, a box of ice cream sandwiches. *Might as well go all out with the junk food.* Voices in the next aisle stopped her in her tracks. It may have been ten years, but she'd recognize the voice of her childhood best friend anywhere.

Dammit. As frozen as the pizza in her basket, Nikki stood and listened but didn't actually hear the words Becky said to the other woman. She absorbed the sound of her friend's voice. Nikki longed to circle around the shelves of cereal and pull the woman who she used to tell everything to into her arms. But common sense prevailed and she snapped out of her daze.

As quietly as she could, she closed the freezer door and was halfway to the till when Nikki remembered her promise to Ryan that he'd be drinking milk with his dinner of junk food. She looked at the basket. *Forget it; there was dairy in the ice cream.*

"Hello there," the cashier said. Nikki loaded the items on the counter and nodded in reply. She glanced at the girl's name tag.

Natalie. She looked about sixteen or seventeen, which meant she would be too young to remember Nikki.

"Is that all for you?" Natalie snapped her gum and stuffed the food into a plastic bag. "We have a two for one on—"

"No. That'll be all."

"Okay." Natalie drew out the word and rolled her eyes.

"Sorry." Nikki handed the girl her credit card. "I'm in sort of a hurry." She snuck a glance towards the back of the store where she'd heard Becky. The aisle was empty.

"No one's ever in a hurry in Halfway," Natalie said. She swiped the card and looked at the name. "It's the slowest town...hey," she said, changing tracks the way teenagers are wont to do. "Are you related to Mrs. Landon? That was a wicked brutal accident. I heard that the car got totally crunched and—"

"I am," Nikki said. She signed her name on the electronic pad and snatched her credit card from Natalie's hand. "She was my mother."

"Oh, oops. My mom's always saying I talk too much, but I…"

Nikki didn't hear anything else the girl said. She turned and fled from the store, desperately needing air. Her eyes burned with the tears that for the last few days she'd held back. She would not cry. Not in front of Ryan.

She stopped for a moment to compose herself before getting back in the car. Ryan was in the backseat, his head still bent over his tablet, totally oblivious of anything going on around him. She usually hated it when he spent so much time on screens and was constantly yanking them away, forcing him to look out the window and take in his surroundings. But as far as she was concerned, for the next few days, he could spend as much time as he wanted playing Minecraft or whatever the current game craze was. It would keep him busy, his mind off losing his grandma, and with any luck, his questions about the town she grew up in to a minimum.

Just a few more days, she told herself. Just long enough to

wrap up her mother's affairs, and put the house up for sale. She'd hire someone to pack it up. The sooner she could get Ryan and herself out of Halfway and back to Seattle, the better. But first, dinner.

Dammit. Nikki looked down at her empty hands. In her haste to get away from the cashier, she'd left her bags behind. For a second, Nikki considered abandoning her purchases and ordering pizza. It would certainly be easier, and it would all but eliminate the chance of running into Becky, who was no doubt still in the store. The only problem with that plan was that as far as she knew, there was nowhere to order pizza in Halfway.

With a sigh, she turned around and walked back into the store. Natalie, looking very apologetic, and blushing all the way to the roots in her hair, had Nikki's bags in her hands and ran over to her.

"I'm so sorry," Natalie said. "I really don't mean to say such stupid things."

"It's okay. It was my fault. I'm really in a hurry and—"

"No way!"

Nikki tightened her grip on the plastic bags and steeled herself. She turned around slowly, and was immediately crushed in a hug.

"Nicole Landon, I should kill you for taking off on me like that." Becky Grant, or rather Jennings now that she's married, was the closest friend she'd ever had, released her from the hug and smacked her lightly on the arm. "But I won't, only because I'm so happy to see you. How are you?" Becky's beautiful smile turned down in a frown and she added, "I'm so sorry about your mom. Such a terrible tragedy. But it did bring you back, and sometimes in times like this, we need to take whatever good we can. When did you get in? I can't even imagine what you're going through…and look at me, not even giving you a chance to speak."

She laughed at herself, and for a moment, Nikki was transported back in time to when they were sixteen. Becky hadn't changed a bit. Opposite in every way to Nikki, Becky was only five foot four. The much taller Nikki had always felt it was a grave injustice. Becky's blond hair was draped down her back, and in jeans and a down-filled coat, she looked exactly the same as the last time Nikki'd seen her. The biggest change was the diamond ring that flashed on her left hand.

Nikki looked away. It wasn't a secret that Becky had married Matt Jennings right after high school. She'd been invited to the wedding, of course. Not that she'd gone.

"I'm doing well," Nikki finally answered. "It's been a hard few days and of course, I have so much to do while I'm here." She hoped maybe that would be enough to get away from any further prying, but Nikki should've known better.

"Of course you do," Becky said. "And one of those things you have to do is come over for dinner. I know Matt will want to see you, too."

Nikki flinched at the mention of his name and hoped Becky didn't notice.

"I really don't know. I mean, I have—"

"I won't take no for an answer." Becky stared at her with those deep green eyes that used to be able to see her secrets. "Besides, you owe me."

The blood drained from her face and for a horrifying second, Nikki thought she might pass out. *There was no way Becky could know. No one knew.*

"Relax," Becky said with a laugh. "You owe me an explanation for where the hell you've been all these years. I'm pissed with you, ya know? You can't just take off and expect me not to be a little upset."

Nikki nodded and relief flooded through her. She glanced back towards the car and Ryan. She needed to hurry. Even with a video game, Ryan wouldn't wait forever without coming in to look for her.

"I know I was a total jerk," she said. "I really am sorry but—"

"Good," Becky said. "Tomorrow night then. It's settled." Becky scribbled her number on a piece of paper and handed it to Nikki before grabbing another wire basket from the stack. "It looks like I have some more shopping to do. Matt will be thrilled when I tell him I ran into you. So, six o'clock? We're at the Jennings' farm. You heard that Matt took over for his dad, right?" Nikki nodded. She remembered well. "Great," Becky continued. "See you then. You remember how to get there?"

She nodded again. "See you then," Nikki muttered, as Becky walked away.

In a daze, she cursed herself all the way to the car, being sure to get in quickly and drive away before she was spotted by anyone else.

"Did you get the pizza, Mom?"

Pasting a smile she didn't feel on her face, Nikki looked into the mirror. "Pepperoni, your favorite."

"You rock, Mom." Ryan smiled, revealing the dimples she loved so much, the ones that never failed to remind her of his father.

CHAPTER 2

~Becky~

BECKY HUMMED to herself as she dropped the bags of groceries into the trunk of her SUV. She couldn't believe Nikki was finally home. It'd been too long. Way too long.

Her fingers drummed on the steering wheel as she pulled out of the Evergreen Grocer parking lot and turned onto the main street. She waved to Mr. and Mrs. Redwood as they ambled across the street ahead of her. She didn't even mind that they seemed to be slower than the turtles in her pond back at the farm today. Nothing was going to ruin the rest of her day: not the Redwoods or the fact that she was going to get stuck at the only red light in a town with no traffic because they took so long to cross the street, nor the fact that she was about to go see Norma, her mother.

Nope. She'd begged for a bit of sunshine in her day today and she got it.

A smile spread across her face as she thought about seeing

Nikki again for the first time in years. She looked good. Better than good, if she were being honest. She looked fabulous. They'd always been polar opposites in their looks. Although Becky was petite and blond and always teased about her doll-like looks, Nikki had been the Amazonian: tall, muscular, and gorgeous with her thick brown hair. Except, back then there'd been no heavy bags beneath the eyes or a forced smile.

Yeah, Becky had caught that smile, but chose to ignore it. She'd make it her goal, her mission to bring the real smile back to Nikki's face, and she knew exactly how to do it, too.

As she pulled into the town's small hospital, Becky mentally sorted through the hundreds of recipes she had and began the process of creating a meal for tomorrow night when the perfect idea hit her. She'd spent the morning trying to come up with a theme for this month's blog posts on her website, Sweet Spoons and Bites. What if she did a Girls Night Out theme? She could start it off with a story about the time she and Nikki had decided to make brownies from scratch one night and came up with a recipe that literally changed Becky's life when she entered it into a contest run by Hershey a few years ago. She could also do a test run of that lava cake recipe she'd found online and post the results tonight on her blog. She was due to post a test recipe on the site, anyways.

She pulled out the bags of food and supplies Norma had demanded she bring today from the back of her vehicle and literally skipped her way up to the front steps of County General.

"Someone's in a good mood today." Dennis Hobs, a local retiree who deemed it his life's mission to greet anyone who came into the hospital with a smile, held the door open for her.

"The sun is shining, I had my coffee already, and Nikki Landon is back in town." Becky planted a quick kiss on Dennis's cheek, something she did every time she ran into her uncle and smiled.

"Well, well, the dynamic duo is back together. I remember the shenanigans you two used to get into." Dennis patted her hand as they walked down the hallway together. "Sad news about her mom, though. Things aren't going to be the same without Marie around to boss your mother about."

"Or the other way around." Becky frowned. "Which reminds me, I'd better hurry…" She lifted up the bags and Dennis waved her away.

County General was a one-floor hospital that consisted of three main areas: the doctors' offices, the patients' wing, and the urgent care center. Becky headed towards the patients' wing where her mother's room was located.

She smiled at the nurses as she walked past and made a quick stop at the nurses' desk to leave a container full of freshly baked chocolate chip cookies. God knows the nurses all deserved a little treat for putting up with Norma this past week.

Becky stood outside the door that led into her mother's private room and took a deep breath. She held it for a few seconds before slowly releasing it. *I will remain calm and cheerful, and not let her get to me. I will remain calm and cheerful—*

"Are you coming in or are you going to stand out there all day?" Norma Grant, yelled.

And not let her get to me. Becky forced a smile on her face. She really couldn't blame her mom for being so cantankerous and obnoxious at the same time. She'd just lost her best friend, she was confined to a hospital bed, and she'd been forced to eat cafeteria food.

Her husband, Matthew, told her that she needed to have an extra dose of patience for her mother right now. And he was right. She did. There could have been two tragic deaths that fateful night, just over a week ago, instead of one. She needed to count her blessings. At least she still had a parent alive, unlike Nikki…

"Your face is all scrunched up," her mother admonished her. "That's how you get wrinkles you know."

Becky just shook her head. "Then don't yell at me." She smiled. "Someone's in a good mood today it seems." Becky placed the bags she'd been carrying on the chair beside the bed and leaned down to kiss Norma's cheek. She was pleased to see some color back in her mother's face. It looked like Sally, the local beautician, had made it in to wash her hair and style it a bit.

"It's hard to be in a good mood in here when all people want to do is poke and prod in places they should just leave alone. It's my hip that is broken, nothing else," her mother grumbled.

"I'm sure they want you out just as much as you want to be out." Becky reached into one of the bags and took out a warm wool cardigan. "I like what Sally did to your hair."

"She did okay." She patted her shoulder-length gray hair before she shook her head. "That's not the one I wanted. I said the green one. That isn't green." Norma's lips pursed together as she leaned forward and let Becky drape the sweater across her back and over her shoulders.

"The green one needed to be washed. I'll bring it in tomorrow." She reached into the bag and pulled out a couple pairs of socks and fingerless mitts. "Before you say anything, I couldn't find the socks you wanted so I brought you some of mine. They have extra layers in them to keep your toes warm."

"I wasn't going to say a word." A hint of a smile appeared on Norma's face as she drew the gloves over her hands and leaned back against her pillow.

Becky unpacked the rest of the items in the bag, placing a book and notepad on the small table beside the bed, along with a smaller container of cookies, and then sat down.

"What did the doctor say this morning?"

Her mother snorted. "It's what the fool didn't say."

"I told you he wouldn't let you out today." As long as she was out by the weekend, that would leave her plenty of time to—

"That's not all…"

Maybe it was the way her mother refused to look at her, or

the way her hands knotted together. Whatever she had to say, it was bad.

"Has she told you she won't be leaving till after the festival?" A deep voice behind Becky broke the news. She twisted in her chair to find Dr. Richard behind her, holding a clipboard in his hand.

That was the news she'd been dreading.

"What do you mean, she can't leave till after the festival?"

"The old fool thinks I'll overdo it so he's keeping me here," Norma muttered.

Becky blinked a few times as she gathered her thoughts. From the disheartened look on her mother's face to the sympathetic smile on Dr. Richard's, Becky figured Norma had already tried to change his mind and failed.

"But…but…" Becky stumbled over her words as the full realization of what the news meant.

She stood and paced the small room. "Who's going to organize the festival this year? It's only a few weeks away and there's still a lot to do. Trust me—I'm the one fielding the calls from everyone wanting to know what's going on."

"Perfect." Dr. Richard stepped into the room and stood beside her chair.

"Excuse me? There's nothing perfect about this situation. This day was supposed to be full of sunshine and happy thoughts. *Happy thoughts.*" Becky pointed at both her mother and the doctor. "Why do I have a feeling you're about to ruin that happiness?"

"Oh, stop being so melodramatic, Rebecca. You'll just have to be the organizer this year and that's that."

Becky looked to Dr. Richard for help but he only shrugged.

"Does she really need to stay here?" Becky didn't even try to hide the whine in her voice.

The older gentleman only nodded while her mother crossed her arms over her chest. "I'm afraid she does. I know your mother too well. She's more stubborn than a mule. She'll do too much and overtax her body and she'll wind back up in here but in worse shape than she is now. Trust me. I know it's the last thing you or the nurses want to hear but she's not going anywhere until after the festival."

Becky's world as she knew it just ended. Although she'd always helped her mother organize the festival, her role barely made a dent in all the behind-the-scenes things her mother and Marie, Nikki's mom, took care of.

"How am I going to do the job of two people? When I offered to help you earlier, it was because you couldn't do it by yourself. Even you admitted that. So how am I supposed to?"

"Oh for Pete's sake." Clearly her mother was more than a little annoyed with her.

For a few seconds, there was silence in the room before Dr. Richard slowly backed out of the room. Becky glared at him for leaving her like this. This was all his fault. When he shut the door behind him, she pursed her lips and turned her attention to her mother.

"I'm sorry but—"

Her mother raised a hand and cut her off. Becky clamped her lips together and counted to three.

"Rebecca Jennings, there is no way that this festival is not going to happen, so pull up your big girl panties and do what needs to be done. It's not like you don't have time. All you do is piddle with recipes and post them online. There's a meeting scheduled for next week with all the participants. The preliminary stuff is done, so you just need to delegate some tasks to all the other volunteers."

"I do more than just piddle," Becky mumbled while she sank down in her chair as the weight of what was entailed rested on her shoulders.

This festival wasn't just a small town gathering. What once used to be a small town tree lighting ceremony had turned into a statewide celebration. Now, there was an annual contest to see which tree farm from the surrounding counties would have the honor of having their tree selected as the tree for the year.

The festival was a whole weekend affair with a winter carnival, food contests, and a plethora of showcase booths from local artisans. This was also the busiest weekend for their family tree farm as families from all over came to select their own personal Christmas tree.

"I'm not in a bad mood," her mother grumbled while a small smile teased her lips. "Okay, maybe a little, but the point is," her mother grabbed her notebook from the small bed table beside her and opened it up, "you won't be doing this alone. I'm here. All you need to do is enlist a couple of your friends to help you with some of the tasks Marie used to take care of and you'll be fine."

"Oh," Becky straightened in the chair, "now that you mention it, you'll never believe who I ran into on my way here?"

Norma opened her eyeglass case and propped her bifocals on the edge of her nose.

"Come on, three guesses." She would love to see a smile on her mother's normally stern face. She used to complain that Nikki was her second daughter because the girls spent so much time together.

"Rebecca…"

Becky hated it when her mother used that tone on her. She felt as if she were back in grade school all over again. "Fine. The least you could have done was attempted a guess." She waited for her mother to look at her. "Nikki's home."

Norma only shrugged. "Well, of course she would be. Someone needs to see to Marie's things. Don't expect her to stick around, though."

"Why not? I've already invited her over for dinner tomorrow night." She planned to do everything she could to delay Nikki returning to wherever she lived now. She knew it was doubtful Nikki would return home for good, but was it too much for her to hope that their friendship could be rekindled? She missed her best friend more than anyone could possibly know.

"Don't get your hopes up, girl. I'd hate to see you get disappointed again."

Becky scooted to the edge of her seat and leaned forward. "I've never believed any of those rumors and you know it."

"One day you'll take off those rose-colored glasses of yours. I just hope you're prepared for a world of hurt when you do."

That was it. She'd had enough of her mother attempting to bring her down. She would let her mother stew in her own self-pity—because that's exactly what it was—and she'd go off and pick up some fresh baked bread from Carla's cafe and get her spaghetti sauce simmering on the stove.

"I'm not naive, Mother. You, of all people, should know that."

She leaned down and laid a soft kiss on her mother's cheek. "I'll be by to see you tomorrow and maybe then we can talk about this festival. Who knows, I might even convince Nikki to help me." She gathered her purse and other bags.

"Don't ask—just tell her she needs to help you. God knows, she owes you that, at least."

CHAPTER 3

❄

~Nikki~

THE NEXT DAY dawned bright and cheery, the exact opposite of Nikki's mood. After setting Ryan up in the guest bedroom the night before, Nikki had gone straight to bed herself. There was so much to do, too much. But she couldn't bring herself to start sorting through her mother's things. Not yet.

As it turned out, she probably should have, for all the sleep she got. Lying in her childhood bed in her old room, she couldn't settle. Too many memories surrounded her. Everywhere she turned, there was another reminder of the life she'd had, the one she'd run from.

As soon as the sun started peeking through the blinds, she'd gotten out of bed, tied her old robe around her, and padded down to the kitchen. There was no point waking Ryan. He needed his sleep. Losing his grandma so suddenly had been difficult for him. On both of them. And that was an understatement.

Her mother had been the only link Nikki had with her past. And the only one who knew the truth.

She went to the cupboard and pulled out the coffee grounds, exactly where her mom had always kept them. She measured out the perfect amount, filled the water, and set it to brew. While she waited, she wandered into the living room. Her mother's knitting sat, half-finished, on the side table next to her chair with a half cup of water. Nikki picked up the yarn, and let it slide through her fingers. She'd been making slippers, probably for Ryan for Christmas.

Tears pricked at Nikki's eyes and her sinuses burned as she tried to hold them back. Ryan needed her to be strong. She was the only one he had now.

Not the only one.

The thought came out of nowhere, surprising her. She shook it away and sniffed loudly. "No," she said aloud. "That's not going to happen."

Even as she said the words, doubt filled her. How could she be back in Halfway and keep her secret? Wasn't that the whole reason she'd left?

She wandered to the mantel and scanned the photos. Most of them were of Nikki and her mother on her visits over the years, with a few of Nikki as a child scattered about. There were none of Ryan. She'd made her mother promise, and she'd kept her word. No one could know about Ryan. Nikki's heart cramped at the hurt it must have caused her mom to hide pictures of her only grandson. Not to mention what Ryan would think if he noticed the absence of photos.

Without thinking, she started gathering the frames off the mantel. Nikki piled them face down on the coffee table and as she reached for the last one, she froze. It was a shot of her and Becky on their prom night. Nikki picked up the picture and walked over to the sofa, where she sank into the cushions.

She remembered exactly when the picture was taken.

They'd decided to get ready at Nikki's house and have the boys pick them up there. Of course, Becky was going to prom with Matt. They'd been together for over a year by that time, with the exception of an important but brief breakup, and were almost completely inseparable. From the moment Becky declared she was interested in Matt, Nikki knew her best friend would get exactly what she wanted. Which was why she'd stepped back and shoved her own feelings for him to the side. Becky was a force of nature when she set her sights on something. And seeing them together, Nikki'd always known she'd made the right decision to back off. They were her closest friends, and they were perfect together.

Nikki had gone to prom with Parker. They'd dated a few times, and he wanted it to be more, but she just couldn't convince herself it was anything serious. He'd been a fun date, though, and prom night was amazing. When the girls had come down the stairs together and her mother had snapped the picture, Nikki had never been happier. Everything was perfect.

After the summer, Becky and Nikki were going to go to college together and be roommates while Matt stayed in the boy's dorm. They were all going to get out of Halfway, and start their lives. Prom night was the celebration of the start of the rest of their lives. Thinking back on that night, Nikki had to blink back the tears that were threatening to spill over. It was one of the best nights of her life. How was she to know that it would be the last night that everything would be okay?

The next day, with her period already two months late, Nikki took the test she'd been putting off. Less than two weeks later, she was gone.

Nikki ran a finger across the glass at the happy girls in the photo. Hadn't she already known on prom night? She was just delaying the inevitable, just as she was doing now. With a sigh, Nikki got up from the couch and went to the phone. She punched in the number Becky had given her the day before and held her breath.

Secretly, she was hoping for the answering machine. *Maybe Becky was still sleeping? What if Matt answered?*

"Shit." She hadn't considered the fact that Matt might answer the phone. She couldn't talk to him. Not yet. Nikki pulled the phone away from her ear and almost hit the button to disconnect when a voice came over the line.

"Hello?"

It was Becky.

"Hello?" Becky said again.

Nikki shook her head and put the phone up to her ear. "Hi, Becky. It's Nikki. Sorry to be calling so early."

"Early?" Becky laughed. "It's not early for me. Not when I have the Tree Festival to singlehandedly organize. Did you know that your mother and my mother always do this together and now with my mother barking orders from the hospital and your mom—oh, Nikki. I'm so sorry. I didn't mean to—"

"It's okay." Nikki turned and stared out the window at the pink sunrise that was making the sky glow. "I know, and it's fine, really," she said and meant it. "So, your mom has you taking over all the planning? Sounds fun."

Unfortunately, Becky missed the sarcasm in her voice and only picked up on the words. "Do you think so? It could be fun," she said. "If you help me."

"What? No, I can't—"

"It'll be fun. The next generation of best friends working together. I was actually going to suggest it, and since you think it's a good idea, too, it'll be perfect."

Nikki shook her head even though Becky couldn't see her. There was no way she could work side by side with her on this. *No way. It wasn't happening.* "I wish I could, Becky," she said. "But I really have so much to do with the house and I can't stay in town very long. I just don't think it would work."

That was an understatement, Nikki thought.

"Please, Nikki. I really need you and you're so good with organizing. Besides, you should stay. It'll be good for you to have a little fun," Becky said. "And didn't I hear that you work from home, anyway? Mom said something about a computer thing."

"I design websites," she said. "But I really can't—"

"We'll talk about it tonight," Becky said as if the matter was settled. "I'm working on this great recipe. Did I tell you about my website? Maybe you could look at it when you come over and give me a few tips?"

Nikki swallowed hard. Becky wasn't going to take it well, but she had to cancel. She couldn't leave Ryan alone and there was absolutely no way she was taking him over to Matt and Becky's house. That wasn't going to happen in a million years. "About tonight," she started. "I'm so sorry, but I just don't think I'm going to be up to it. I'm a little overwhelmed with everything I have to do here at the house and to make arrangements and everything. I just don't think it's a good idea, tonight."

"Oh."

"It's not that I don't want to," Nikki added quickly. Becky always was sensitive when she canceled plans, and the last thing Nikki wanted was to make her old friend feel worse. If she wasn't careful, there'd be a lot more hurt coming for everyone before she left town. "I do, Becky. I just don't think it's a good idea tonight. I need to get things packed up is all."

"Well, if you're sure."

"I'm sorry, Becky."

"It's okay. Maybe we can do it in a few days?" She heard Becky take a deep breath on the other end of the line. "Oh, and speaking of packing up, I thought you might need a few more boxes, so I had Matt load them up in the truck for you."

A knot of panic formed in Nikki's chest.

"He said he'd bring them over for you later," Becky continued.

"That's not necessary." Nikki turned when she heard a creak

on the stairs. Ryan, still in his pajamas, his blond hair mussed and standing up at strange angles, was walking downstairs, rubbing his eyes. She held up her finger to her lips. "Really, Becky. I don't need any boxes. I'm good and I don't want to trouble Matt with anything. I know how busy he must be at this time of year. The last thing he needs is to be coming all the way out here on a silly errand."

Becky chuckled, totally oblivious of the rising panic Nikki was feeling. "It's no trouble at all," she said. "He's actually on his way over right now. He had to run out and grab some coffee from Grounds since I forgot to pick some up yesterday. So he said he'd run over right away before you got started packing. We both thought you'd be up and at it already."

Nikki spun around, unsure of what she was looking for. *Matt couldn't come here. No.* Ryan sat at the table and plopped his tired head in his hands. "Becky, I have to go. I'll talk to you soon, okay?"

"Okay, maybe I'll—"

Nikki hung up on whatever it was Becky was going to say. She couldn't think. She ran her hands through her hair and pulled at the roots. If Matt was on his way over, he would be there soon. She didn't have much time. She needed to do something. Anything. Her heart raced. A bead of sweat broke over her brow and she grabbed the counter to support herself because she wasn't sure her legs could hold her up for another moment.

"Mom?"

Ryan.

Through a veil of hair, she looked at her son. She had to get a hold of herself. She couldn't fall apart, not now. She took a deep breath. She was strong. She'd been through worse. She could make it through this. With a deep breath, she stood up straight and pushed away from the counter.

"I'm fine, Ryan." She walked over to him and ruffled his hair. "Did you sleep okay? You look tired." She forced a lightness into her voice and hoped he didn't notice as she glanced out the window. If Matt was going to stop by, maybe she could head him off at the door.

"Why don't you have some cereal for breakfast?" She opened the cupboard on the off chance that her mom had some cereal that wasn't totally bran. She pulled out a box of Cheerios. "Here you go."

Everything was exactly where she remembered it and it only took a few seconds for her to find a bowl and a spoon. Ryan was happily munching away when she heard the truck pull into the driveway. Her heart automatically picked up the pace and Nikki had to force herself to calm down. She picked up her coffee cup, took a sip and slowly walked to the kitchen door.

"Hey, buddy?" Ryan lifted his head, the spoon halfway to his mouth. "I'm just going to be outside for a second, okay? You just finish your breakfast. I'll be in in a second, okay?"

Ryan shrugged and continued to eat, so Nikki slipped from the room, walked through the living room and opened the front door just as Matt was pulling a stack of folded cardboard from the back of his pick-up. She closed the door behind her and gripped the coffee mug to keep her hands from shaking. She wasn't ready. It'd been so long.

And then, he turned. His eyes met hers and she started at the familiar deep blue. When his face split into a smile, and his dimples deepened into his cheeks, Nikki shook so violently, hot coffee spilled onto her hand.

She wiped it on her pants and forced a smile to her face. "Hi, Matt."

"Nikki." He all but sprinted up the stairs to the porch, balancing the awkward stack of boxes. "It's so good to see you." She knew he meant it, too. Matt didn't have an insincere bone in his body. "I'm so sorry about your mom." His smile faltered. "What a tragedy it all was, and…well, it shouldn't have happened. I'm so sorry."

"Thanks, Matt," she said. "That means a lot."

"I'm glad you're back, though. I really want to give you a hug." He jostled the boxes around again, trying to shift them to one arm. "Is there somewhere I can drop these for you?"

"No."

Matt looked at her and raised an eyebrow. "You don't need them?"

"I...um..." Nikki desperately searched her brain for something to tell him. "I do," she said finally, because anything else would be a lie and he'd know it.

"Okay." He drew the word out slowly. "Let me take them inside for you."

"No," she said with a little more force than she intended. When Matt tilted his head and gave her a strange look, she added, "That's fine. You can just leave them on the porch." She put her coffee mug down and moved a chair, trying to clear a place. "Here, I'll just move a few—"

"Nonsense," Matt said. "I'll just take them in." Before Nikki could stop him, he shifted the load to his left hand and used his right to open the door and all she could do was pick up her coffee mug and helplessly follow him inside.

"Just put them here," she said. Nikki glanced in the direction of the kitchen and said a silent prayer that Ryan was having a second helping of cereal.

Matt dropped the boxes and straightened up. Before she could object, he wrapped his arms around her and squeezed. Her coffee sloshed over the side, splashing on both of them, but Matt didn't seem to care. He only pulled her tighter. "It really is good to see you, Nikki." He spoke into her hair and she closed her eyes, fighting the overwhelming rush of emotions that were crashing into her just by being close to him.

She tried to wiggle out of his embrace. "Matt, I—"

"I've missed you, Nik," he said, using his nickname for her. "It hasn't been the same, since—"

"Mom?"

Her blood drained from her face, and if Matt hadn't been holding on to her, she would have fallen over. For an instant the world stopped, and there was nothing but a roar in her head. Matt released her, and only by instinct, she grabbed the couch to hold herself up. She watched as Matt's face changed from shock to slow realization as he took in the miniature version of himself that stood before him.

Seeing them together, it was undeniable. From their mussed blond hair, to their ice blue eyes and the matching dimples in their cheeks.

In slow motion, Nikki turned to face Ryan. "Hey, buddy. Can you go back in the kitchen? I just need to finish talking to…Mr. Jennings. I'll be done in a minute."

"Wait," Matt said. "You have a son." It wasn't a question, but there was something in his voice that asked a lot more.

She nodded but wouldn't look at him.

"Nikki," he spoke softly, but firmly. "How old is he?"

She shook her head, willing Matt to take his questions and go away. She focused on her son. "Go finish breakfast, Ryan." She kept her face as neutral as possible until he left the room.

"Nikki," Matt said again. "How old?" He grabbed her shoulder and spun her around so she was facing him. Despite the questions on his lips, there was no denying the clarity in his eyes. Matt was a smart man and it wouldn't take a genius to figure out what was plain for anyone to see. "Tell me, Nikki," he said, giving her shoulders a small shake.

Tears pricked her eyes, but she forced them away. There was no room for that. Not now. She took a deep breath and set her jaw before she said, "Do I really need to answer that?"

CHAPTER 4

~*Becky*~

BECKY SAT down at her office desk and turned her computer on. She checked her phone again to see whether Matt had texted her back since she'd first sent him a message to pick up some sugar while grabbing the coffee. That had been an hour ago. He should have been home by now. *How long did it take to drop off boxes?*

Instead of the coffee she craved, she sipped on a cup of homemade hot chocolate with shaved milk chocolate, cocoa, sugar, and heavy cream that she'd simmered on the stove. She'd been trying out a few variations of the homemade mix because she wanted to use these as gifts in some gift baskets she was going to give out on her website and to friends and family around town. So far, this one was the best recipe she'd tried—except it could use a little bit more sugar.

She had a list of things to accomplish today but she couldn't get motivated. All she could think about was how Nikki couldn't hide the fact she'd wanted to get off the phone with her. She knew, no matter what Nikki had said, that she would never come over for dinner, and there was no doubt in her mind that she was trying to figure out how to get out of town as quickly as she could before Becky found out.

Well, that wasn't going to happen. Not again.

Back in high school, they'd both had dreams and aspirations. Being the wife of a tree farmer wasn't exactly what Becky had in mind when she thought about her future, but then neither had being a baker with her own cookbook and a growing fan base. She'd wanted to explore the world, to experience history firsthand and maybe even become an anthropologist. Anything that would take her away from Halfway and her mother.

But then Nikki had vanished just as summer began and Matt's father had his first stroke. Heading off to college alone wasn't something Becky had wanted to do and with Nikki gone...she'd felt alone. When Matt broke the news that he had to enroll in the local college and help out more with the family farm, Becky had made the impulse decision to do the same. They married a month after graduation.

"Funny how plans change," Becky muttered to herself as she scrolled through a social media site and looked at the recent baby photos one of her online followers had posted. Becky made a mental note to post some homemade baby food recipes and diet-friendly desserts.

Her heart ached as she paused on an image of the mother holding her child close. Being a mother was a dream Becky had always had, but after multiple miscarriages, she'd finally let go of that wish. Matt had broached the subject of adoption, but she wasn't sure she was ready for that. Her last miscarriage had only been a few months ago and the pain was still too...fresh.

She closed the browser and leaned back in her chair. They'd been so close last time, almost making it to the twelve-week mark, the longest she'd ever carried one of her babies. Her gaze strayed to the bookshelf in her office where she kept the journals she'd bought after each pregnancy. The first book, with a soft cream cover, was full of her hopes and dreams for their child. Every feeling, every sensation, even every episode of morning sickness was recorded. Then, after that miscarriage, every tear, heartbreak, and question for God was recorded. She'd bought another journal for her second pregnancy, but this time her joy was more reflective and the pages were full of prayers for a healthy pregnancy. In total, there were four journals. She didn't think she could handle buying another one, even if it were for an adopted child.

She heard the sound of a door slamming and pushed herself up from the chair. Finally, Matt was home. She went to see whether he needed help with the grocery bags but he came into the house empty-handed and walked past her with barely a word.

"Matt?"

He turned to look at her, but it was as if he saw right through her.

"Are you okay?" He gave his head a little shake but didn't say anything. "Did you get the coffee and sugar?"

"Sugar?" His shoulders deflated.

"I sent you a text." She knew he got it. It showed as read on her phone.

"Yeah, sorry...I totally forgot. I can go back into town and get it later, okay?" He sank down on a bar stool at their kitchen counter and pulled his phone out of his pocket.

"I kind of needed it now. Nikki canceled dinner tonight"—Matt's head popped up—"so I thought I'd make her something and take it into her. Maybe help her pack."

"No. I mean..." Matt shook his head. "I'll take it in."

Becky grabbed a recipe book off the shelf of her curio cabinet and thumbed through the pages. "Why? I thought you told me this morning you needed to be down in the field for the day, which is why you went into town this morning for me."

"Do you think that's a good idea?"

She lifted her gaze from the recipe book to her husband and noticed that he wasn't looking at her. "Why wouldn't it be?"

He licked his lips before pocketing his phone and rose. "Nikki...I think she just wants to be left alone."

Becky winced at his words. "What she wants and what she needs are two different things. She just lost her mother—being alone right now isn't what she needs. She needs to know she's still loved and accepted and that the past is behind us." She leaned her elbows down on the counter. "We were best friends, Matt. Best friends. No matter what happened that drove her away, that has never changed."

She watched as her husband stepped towards her and held out his arms. She gladly went into them. She loved the feel of his arms around her, knowing how safe and protected she was.

"Sometimes the past is best left alone," he whispered into her hair before he laid a kiss on her forehead.

Becky looked up into his eyes and was confused by what she saw in there. Fear, hope, uncertainty. His forehead knitted together before he blinked and pulled away.

"Oh trust me, I don't plan to dredge up the past. I'm just happy she's back. I plan to do all I can to make sure she knows it, too." Becky smiled as an idea came to her.

"What?" Matt must have recognized the look in her eyes.

"All Nikki needs to know is that she's not alone, and I know the perfect way to prove that."

Matt shook his head. "Becky, I don't think—"

She held up her hand to stop him. "Trust me, okay?" It would work. All Nikki needed was a reason to stay. One person can't change all that much. Nikki was always the type to step in when someone needed help, whether it was someone needing a last-minute babysitter or a volunteer at the hospital.

Well, Becky needed her to help with the Tree Festival. But that wasn't all. She knew the perfect way for Nikki to use her computer skills to help not only the festival but the town itself.

Now all she needed to do was convince her best friend of this.

###

BECKY PUSHED OPEN the door to the *Halfway Herald* front office and breathed in the deep scent of aspen pine. A large tree sat in the middle of the large front window but the floor around it was strewn with opened boxes of tree ornaments. Melissa Trait, owner of the paper, stood behind the counter and handed a stack of printed flyers to her daughter.

"This time, make sure you leave only one in each mailbox." Melissa frowned as her daughter plugged her ears with plugs that blared with music from her iPod. "Shay, I mean it." Her daughter stuffed the papers into her backpack and almost knocked into Becky as she rushed out the front door.

"I swear, sometime that kid will be the death of me," Melissa mumbled as she watched her daughter cross the street with her head down, barely noticing the car that slowed down for her to cross. Melissa grabbed a small shoe box from the counter and held it out.

Becky reached for it. "I can't believe how big she's gotten." Melissa had been left to raise her daughter when her husband skipped town a few years ago. Being a single mother hadn't been easy for Melissa, and Becky was so thankful she wasn't in her shoes.

"Yesterday she stuffed twenty flyers into ten mailboxes. Twenty! The phone rang all day with people complaining. All she wants to do is listen to her music and hang out with her friends." Melissa's arms folded across her ample chest as she stared out the window until her daughter was out of sight.

"She's a kid. I remember us being like that too. In fact"—Becky juggled the box she held in her hands until she was able to get her purse off her shoulder and place it on the counter—"I seem to remember helping you burn a few hundred flyers your father gave you to pass out into mailboxes a few times."

"The trouble I used to get in..." The expression on Melissa's face softened as her shoulders relaxed and she turned towards Becky. "I've been trying to decorate this tree all morning." She glanced down at the box in Becky's hands. "You can help."

Becky rolled her eyes at the command but opened the box to reveal a variety of small glass ornaments in the shape of Christmas trees in the box. "I thought you had the trees last year?"

It had become a tradition years ago, back when her mother had taken over organizing the yearly festival, to have a town ornament created in the shape of a tree. One class from the elementary school would design it and one store along Main Street would host the tree adorned with all the ornaments.

"Your mom never got around to assigning which store got the tree this year, so I figured I'd just put it up again. How's she doing, by the way?"

Becky shrugged. "You know Mom. She's giving Dr. Richard a hard time for keeping her in the hospital until the festival is over. I totally forgot she did that every year—assign the tree to a different store, I mean."

"Well, who else would do it? It's part of the festival. Which reminds me," Melissa's lips quirked, "who's going to run it this year?"

"Me." Becky pursed her lip. The first tree she'd pulled out of the box was the one she'd designed back in grade six. She turned the tree over and searched for her initials she'd placed on the star and smiled at the memory of how much trouble she'd gotten into that year for doing that. She smiled at the memory. The star on the top of the ornament was always to remain unadorned and was to look like the tree they used each year to top their town tree, but that year, just before her teacher had submitted the design, Becky had scribbled her initials at the tip of one of the star points.

"You?" Doubt filled her friend's tone.

She rolled her neck to get rid of a kink. "I'll need help, of course."

"Of course. Your mother and Marie Landon were the dynamic duo when it came to this festival. Between the two of them, nothing dared to go wrong. Such a shame what happened." Melissa sighed. "You know, your mother usually had the flyers all prepared by now." Melissa stepped away from the tree and reached over the old oak counter and pulled out a large scrapbook from beneath. It contained every single flyer ever printed, a practice her father had started when he began the *Halfway Herald*.

Becky rummaged through her purse and pulled out a notebook. "Flyers. Right. That's on the list."

Melissa's brows rose. "It should be at the very top of the list. Becky, you need to get those out, right and quick. I'd offer to do them but I'm up to my eyeballs in other work and Lorraine is on holidays."

Becky was surprised to hear this. Lorraine was one of those women who was always around and the type to fill in anywhere and everywhere. She'd pitch in for Sunday School classes if someone didn't show up, she'd volunteer at the community center, help the local florist with deliveries, drop by someone's home and bring a meal if they were sick...Lorraine pretty much never left town.

"Lorraine never takes a vacation. Where did she go?"

"Her daughter showed up last week and literally dragged her away. Something about a fourteen-day cruise." She sighed. "If anyone deserved a vacation, it's Lorraine. But it was last minute and left me in the lurch."

Becky bit back her smile. *This was perfect.*

"So basically, I need someone to take on the design aspect for this festival. Anything other than the flyers?"

Melissa tapped her chin with a pen. "Well, there's the ad I put in the paper, the notices that go up all over town..."

Becky leaned forward. "What about a website?"

Melissa shook her head. "Our town website hasn't been updated in...years. I know Norma has talked about having a website created for the festival but no one ever volunteered to take it on."

Becky plucked the pen out of Melissa's hand and jotted down a few notes in her book. "What if I said I knew of someone who could update this for us?"

"Do you now?" A smile grew across Melissa's face. Becky knew she was thinking of all the different ways an updated website could be used.

"I do. And just think—that spotlight you always wanted on the town's website for upcoming news and a community calendar, well, she could probably do that too." All that and more. Why, it would probably become a full-time position, keeping the town's website up and running. Halfway might be a little town stuck in the middle of nowhere but that didn't mean nothing happened around here.

"She? Who do you know that could do this? You know the council already squashed the idea of hiring an outside firm to do this. They want it to be someone local."

Becky nodded. Maintaining local resources was crucial to the town's wellbeing.

"Well, spill. Who could do this?"

Becky let out a long sigh. She knew this plan would work. It had to.

"Let's just say an old friend is back in town and she just happens to run a website design company."

Melissa wasn't just the owner of the town's only newspaper. She was also one of the busiest gossips around. Once word spread that there was someone in town will skills that could help the community...there was no way Nikki could leave.

CHAPTER 5

~*Nikki*~

AFTER MATT LEFT, Nikki followed him out to the porch. To do what? She didn't know. When he realized the truth, Nikki'd seen it cross his face. But he didn't say anything. He'd just stared at Ryan before turning and storming out without a word.

She'd left Ryan standing in the living room while she went to watch as Matt got in his truck and spun out of her drive. She didn't call out to him or try to explain. And even if he had stayed, there was nothing she could say to him. An apology wasn't enough, and after ten years, what was the point?

"Mom?" Ryan startled her and she broke out of her daze. Her son looked at her with his father's eyes, and just as it always did when she looked at him, she felt the flicker of sorrow. Only this time, the feeling was magnified. "Who was that?"

She reached out and brushed the hair off his forehead. "Just an old friend."

"Do I know him?"

She shook her head and forced a small smile. "No." Nikki paused. "No, you don't know him."

She knew coming home to Halfway was a risk. She knew there was a chance of Matt finding out. Or Ryan asking questions. But there hadn't been a choice. She'd had to come home. And now all she could do was finish up and leave town as quickly as possible. "Come on," she said, and grabbed Ryan's hand. "I bet Grandma had some cookies or something in the freezer."

She led Ryan back into the kitchen, and distracted him with baked goods, which she knew would work. At least for a little while. Ryan barely got any fresh baking, unless her mother had come to visit. She couldn't seem to get anything to turn out, so she stuck to store bought—it was safer that way.

With her son settled for the moment in front of the television, Nikki got to work. She only had a few days to clear up whatever details she could and then she needed to go. Especially now that Matt knew the truth, the faster she could get finished up, the better.

In the kitchen, she flipped through her mother's papers until she found the town directory, right where it'd always been kept. She dialed the number for the funeral home and leaned against the counter, giving herself a moment to close her eyes before Levi Jenkins picked up.

"Levi? It's Nicole Landon. I'm calling—"

"Nikki. I've been expecting your call. I'm so sorry about your mother. She was a fine lady." The familiar voice washed over her, soothing her frayed nerves. There was a reason Levi owned the only funeral home in town. There was something so naturally comforting about him, you couldn't help but feel better in his presence. He also had the strangest resemblance to Santa Claus, and even when Nikki was a child, she'd thought he was old enough to be her grandfather. But he was still in Halfway, and for that, Nikki was grateful.

"Thank you, Levi." She swallowed the sadness that she didn't have time for. "There's so much to do," she said. "I suppose I'll need to come by and take care of some details."

"That's not necessary, Nikki. You mother took care of everything before her passing. She said that she wanted to make it as easy for you as possible, because she wasn't sure if you'd come back to town in the event of her passing."

A flash of guilt and surprise went through her. "What?"

"I didn't ask for the details," Levi said. "After all, that's not my job. But she seemed set on taking care of the details, so it's all arranged. All I need from you is an outfit for the—"

"Okay." Nikki nodded her head, still trying to process what he'd said. "I can do that. And since there won't be a service, I'll—"

"Oh, there'll be a service."

"But, I have to—"

"Your mother wanted a service, Nikki," Levi said, firmly. "And that's what she'll get. I have her requests for music and flowers and—"

"But, I really can't stay. I don't think it will—"

"Nicole Landon. Your mother was not only a valued customer, but she was also one of my dear friends, and if she wanted a service, that is what she'll get and given the timing, I've scheduled it for Friday."

Nikki's head spun and she rubbed her eyes for a moment before looking at the calendar her mother had hanging on the wall. "Friday? But that's almost a week away." Her finger found the day. And the bold words written in the square next to it. "And the day before the Tree Festival."

"Yes," Levi said. "I think she'd like that, don't you?"

Nikki nodded despite the fact he couldn't see it. "Yes, she would. But—"

"Good. Then it's settled. I'll need the outfit whenever you can find it. I look forward to seeing you, Nikki."

She hung up the phone and stared at it for a moment before

returning her gaze to the calendar. The Tree Festival? A week away. She couldn't stay in Halfway for an entire week.

Nikki gave herself one more minute to feel sorry for herself before springing into action. If her mother wanted a service, there was no way she was going to resist it. She'd been selfish enough where her mother was concerned and Lord knows her mom had sacrificed more than enough where Nikki was concerned.

She peeked in on Ryan in the living room. He seemed settled enough, watching cartoons. "I'm going to start packing," she said. He only raised his hand in recognition, but didn't move. "Ryan?" She took a few steps towards him. "Are you okay?"

Nikki perched on the arm of the sofa and tried to stroke his blond hair but he jerked away.

"I'm good."

She tried not to be hurt. It wasn't like him to pull away from her. "I know it's been hard, buddy. You know if you want to talk, you can come to me, right?"

He turned to her. "I know, Mom. I'm fine. Honestly. I'm just watching TV."

Her motherly instincts were on high alert, but she knew better than to push it. "Okay," she said after a moment. Nikki smacked her palms on her lap and pushed up from the couch. "I'll be upstairs if you need me."

She took one more look at him before she made her way up the stairs. His gaze didn't leave the screen, so she shook her head and went up to her mother's room.

###

HER MOTHER'S room looked exactly the way Nikki remembered it. As if she hadn't changed a thing since she'd been a child. The smell of her mom's vanilla-scented perfume hung in the air and for a moment, Nikki closed her eyes and let the familiar scent wash over her. Tears burned her eyes and she swiped at them.

"No," she said aloud. "I can't do this now." She wouldn't let herself fall apart. Not when there was so much to do. She couldn't.

The wall on the far side of the room caught Nikki's attention. That was different from the last time she'd been home. She moved closer to look at what was a photo wall dedicated to Ryan. Pictures from when he was a baby, all the way up to the most recent shot Nikki had mailed of Ryan on his bike, covered in mud after getting caught out in a storm. Each picture was framed and hung neatly.

She couldn't hold the tears back and her heart broke at the thought of her mom having to hide her only grandson away from her friends in such a way. Nikki ran her fingers down the frames, one at a time, pausing at a photo of Ryan and his grandma that she herself had taken the last time she'd come to visit.

"Oh, Mom. I'm so sorry." She took the photo off the wall and hugged it to her chest.

Never once had her mom complained or protested about Nikki's choice to keep Ryan a secret. Even when Nikki told her the truth about who Ryan's father was. But not once had Nikki ever considered how hard keeping the secret would have been for her mom. She'd been incredibly selfish. She knew that. She'd always known that. But she'd also done it for a reason. For Becky. The truth would destroy her best friend.

And they were best friends. Despite Nikki's poor choices and everything that had come after. A friend of the heart didn't just go away because there was distance between you. Becky couldn't know the truth.

But Matt knew.

Nikki shook her head, trying to block the reality she needed to face.

Putting the photo down, she sniffed and wiped her eyes with the back of her hand. She needed to pull herself together. Without another look at the picture wall, Nikki went to the closet and selected a beautiful blue skirt and jacket set. It would be a lovely color for her mom. And it wasn't black, which her mother would have hated.

She went to the jewelry box on the dresser to choose some jewelry when a voice startled her.

"Who was that man?"

Nikki jumped and then froze when Ryan's words sank in. Something in the way he asked got her attention.

She turned slowly and looked at him. "I told you," she said. "He's just an old friend."

"I feel like I know him." Ryan didn't look at her when he spoke. Instead, he walked to the far side of the room and stared at the wall of pictures.

She watched him as he looked at each of the pictures, but she didn't say anything. She waited until he turned to her and spoke again. "I do know him," he said. "Don't I?"

She didn't make it a practice to lie to her son. In fact, Nikki had always believed it was best to be as honest with Ryan as possible. Except for one area. In that, she couldn't tell him the truth. She'd always told Ryan his dad was from her town but had moved away and they'd lost touch. How could she tell him the truth about who his father was and then explain why he couldn't see him? It wasn't an option. It never had been. Until now.

Nikki took a breath and assessed her son, so much like his father it couldn't be denied for much longer. "Ryan." She shook her head. "I don't think—"

"Why won't you tell me the truth?" The anger behind his words startled her and she took a step back. "I know that I know him, Mom. And I know that you're lying to me."

"Ryan." She took a step towards him, wanting to close the gap between them. They'd always been so close. A team. But in only a few days, she could feel the distance between them. It was Halfway. It was this place. Being home. The secrets. The lies. "I need you to understand, buddy." She reached out to touch him, but he pulled away.

"I'm not a kid anymore, Mom."

She wanted to smile. He was still a kid. After all, he was only ten. And that still meant he was a kid, didn't it? She opened her mouth, but couldn't find the words to tell him what she knew he wanted to hear.

His eyes traveled back to the wall and Nikki watched while his focus changed and he fell apart. "I miss her, Mom." Ryan's head fell and his shoulders started to shake with the tears she knew he had to have been holding in.

In one step, she was at his side, and had her arms wrapped around him. There were still so many questions she didn't know how to answer. But comfort was one thing she could give.

"I know, Ryan," Nikki said as she rubbed his back. "I miss her, too. So much."

She let him cry for a few minutes, because sometimes that's what needed to be done. And when his sobs began to subside, she pulled away and wiped his tears with her thumb. "It's not fair that we had to lose her," she said. "But you have to know that Grandma loved you more than anything else in the world. You know that, right?"

He nodded.

Nikki reached past him to the bed and picked up the photo she'd dropped their earlier. "In fact," she said. "Why don't we take this picture downstairs and put it on the mantel while we're here? Would you like that?"

Ryan nodded and wiped his nose with the back of his arm.

"I think Grandma would have liked that, too. Very much."

CHAPTER 6

❄

~Becky~

BECKY PULLED up in front of Nikki's mother's front walkway and looked out her window. She knew coming unannounced was a risky move to make, but she needed to have a plan in place for the festival before she headed over to the hospital to see her mother. This was her chance to prove to Norma that…that what? That she was better than the typical wife who stayed home and cooked all day? Not once had her mother acknowledged what Becky had accomplished in her life. Instead, all she heard about was how she threw her dreams away for love. It was almost as if having her own cookbook published was beneath her.

No matter what she did, it always felt like she could never earn her mother's approval. Didn't mean she wouldn't keep trying, though.

Her phone vibrated in the cup holder with a text from Matt.
Heading to north corner in back field. Will be late.
That was odd. There was nothing back there. That back field

was being left alone for another year, to give the ground some rest before they planted more trees. He should be in their southern fields, marking the trees for customers to cut down. They only had a week left before the gates opened for the season.

Her fingers tapped the phone. *Something wrong?* Her mind raced with possible scenarios of what would take him back there. There was a neighboring farm off that lot, but they'd never had issues in the past.

Just checking out the old cabin. See you for dinner.

Becky shook her head at his text. That old cabin needed to be torn down but Matt wouldn't hear of it. His great-grandfather had built that cabin, the original homestead, back in the day. Matt's father had left it alone, using it as an old camping site for the local Boy Scout group in Halfway. A few years ago, Matt had put a stop to that as the cabin fell apart and was unsafe. He'd started talking about fixing it up again and making it livable. They could rent it out to groups or campers, adding another source of income. But that was a project for the spring, not a week before the tree-cutting season was to start.

She gathered her purse, stuffing her phone inside, and opened her door. She'd made a casserole for Nikki to reheat for dinner and had grabbed an apple pie from Sweet 'n Savory, the local bakery. She would have made it herself, but without the sugar…it wouldn't have been worth it.

As she walked up the front walkway, Nikki met her on the porch with a guarded look on her face.

"Since you won't come to my house for dinner, I brought dinner to you." Becky held out the casserole dish and waited for the deer-in-headlights look to fade from Nikki's gaze.

"You didn't have to do that." Nikki stared at the dish but didn't reach for it.

"I know. But it beats the frozen pizza you probably would have eaten, right?" She set the casserole dish down on the wicker table by the front door when it became evident that Nikki wasn't going to take it and pushed her hands deep into her jacket pockets.

From the way Nikki stood guard in front of the front door, it was a good thing the weather had warmed up. Becky zipped up her jacket and then sat down on the porch swing.

"Remember when we used to sit out here for hours during the summer? We'd daydream about our futures and how we were going to change the world?"

"That's not quite how I remember it."

Becky hid her smile as her friend finally moved away from the door and sat down in the chair opposite her.

"Really?"

"We'd sit out here for hours only because you were too scared to book it home and face the wrath of your mother once she caught wind of your shenanigans."

Becky's brow rose. "Shenanigans? Really, Nik? You sound just like both our mothers combined right there."

Nikki shrugged. "You were always getting into some sort of trouble."

Becky shook her head as she leaned back. "And yet I was never alone." She winked and was pleased to see a smile grace her friend's face. Between the two of them, Becky had been the more adventurous type but Nikki always tagged along for the ride.

"We had a lot of fun, didn't we?" The smile left Nikki's face as she gazed into the front window of her mother's home.

"We did. It's too bad it had to end, especially the way it did."

An uncomfortable silence grew between them. Becky had hoped maybe Nikki would apologize and attempt to give some sort of explanation of why she left…but she didn't. In fact, she just sat there, refusing to even look at her.

Becky sighed. *Fine then.* "Do you need help?" The front room held the boxes Matt had brought by earlier.

Nikki shook her head. "I'm good. But thank you."

Becky caught the way her hands gripped the edge of the seat.

"Good," she said, forcing a lighthearted tone to her voice. "'Cause I need your help and I'll do anything, even bribe you with meals, if that's what it will take."

There was a look in Nikki's eyes, as if she were about to bolt. Becky leaned forward and took a deep breath. She had no idea what was going on, but she needed to figure out a way to keep Nikki seated and hopefully get her talking.

"Listen, I know now probably isn't the best timing, but I could really use your help with this festival."

Nikki snorted. "You do realize how long it's been since I was even at the festival, right?"

"I know, I know. But just hear me out." She pulled out her notepad. "The festival is one week away and I just found out today that I need to create a flyer and design an ad for the town paper. Except, I have no idea how to do any of that."

The skeptical look on Nikki's face told her what she thought of that.

"I bake and cook. That's as far as my talents go. But you…you do websites, so you must be good at graphics, right? We don't need anything fancy. And here," she pulled out samples she'd gotten from Melissa earlier, "this is all my mother did last year for the paper. And then this was the flyer." She unfolded the copy Melissa had made for her and spread it out for Nikki to see.

"As easy as those look, I really don't think I'll have the time. I want to put this house up on the market as soon as possible and Mom's funeral is on Friday."

Becky straightened. "Friday?" The timing couldn't be more perfect. "That's the day before the festival."

"Yeah. Mom had it all planned out, I guess, and Levi thought it would be a nice touch."

"Leave it to Levi. You know he had a crush on her, right?"

"He did not!" Nikki's eyes grew round moments before she started to chuckle. "She never said a word."

"I doubt she knew. I overheard Norma tease him a few years ago about it."

Nikki's grip on the chair relaxed. "Could you imagine having Santa as a stepfather?"

"The kids love him, that's for sure. I'm not sure what this town will do when he's not around to put on the red suit. You should see him in action these past few years. Do you remember Elizabeth Preening? She married Derek Banner a year after I married Matt. Anyways, she picked up photography as a hobby and it turns out she's pretty good at it. She does it for a living now—has her own shop just off the main street and takes all the Santa photos with the kids now."

There was nothing Becky had loved more, in the past, than to watch those little kids see Santa up close and have their picture taken with him. The expression of wonder on their faces…and the smile on Levi's. She'd once overheard him say to her mother that there was nothing more worthwhile to him than to see someone smile at him with joy rather than with sorrow.

"Hopefully he'll be around long enough for you to get your babies' pictures taken." Nikki glanced away from her and stared down at the porch floor. "I thought you would have had a few of your own by now."

Becky sighed. "So did I." She blinked past the tears that gathered in her eyes.

Sitting there, with Nikki again, brought back so many memories. Despite the distance between them, there was still a bond. She thought back to all the times when she'd wished Nikki were with her, to help her get through all the hard times. She hadn't really realized just how much she missed not having her there.

"One day, though, right?" There was a desperate sound of hope in Nikki's voice. Almost as if she knew that something was wrong.

Becky shook her head. "I don't think so. My body doesn't seem to like the idea of having children, no matter how many times we've tried. I've had a few…miscarriages. Matt would like to adopt one day." Becky sucked in a deep breath. "We'll see. He'd make a wonderful father and there's nothing he wants more in life than to be a dad."

And yet, the thought of adopting, as wonderful as it was, made her feel like she'd failed in some way. Like she wasn't good enough to be a mother. Maybe the miscarriages were her body's way of telling her that.

"I'm so sorry." Nikki's voice dropped into almost a whisper. "I had no idea. My mom never said anything."

"Probably because she didn't know." That was one thing her and Matt did agree upon: keeping her miscarriages a secret. They didn't want the pitying looks from everyone. Norma knew about the first two losses, but that was it. After that, they'd agreed to wait until she'd passed the three-month mark before they told anyone.

Nikki's face had completely drained of color, almost to the point where Becky thought she'd pass out. "What's wrong? Are you okay?"

Nikki held up her hand, stopping Becky as she rose from her chair. "I'm fine. I'm fine. I just…I never knew. I just assumed you were waiting. You'd always said you wanted to focus on a career before kids, so I just thought…"

Becky's shoulder muscles tightened. "Things change. I'd also wanted to be an archeologist and never thought children would fit into my lifestyle. Now I'm a tree farmer's wife, living in a house with empty bedrooms that should be full of childish laughter." She frowned. "Fate has a funny way of playing tricks on a person."

A sudden breeze blew through the porch and Becky shivered. When Nikki glanced down at her watch, Becky got the impression that it was time to leave.

"Listen, no matter what happened between us, I could really

use your help right about now. Please?" Nikki was her only option at this point. Time was running out.

"Nothing happened between us. Life just got in the way," Nikki whispered. She reached for the flyer Becky had set down on the table between them. "Sure, I can help. This won't take me long and will give me a break from packing. Why don't I work on it tonight and forward it to Melissa by morning? That should give her enough time to do whatever she needs to do with it, right?"

A wave of relief swept over Becky at Nikki's words.

"Thank you. Seriously, you are my lifesaver. And I was serious about the casseroles. Consider your meals taken care of while you do what needs to be done." Becky stood and grabbed her purse. She'd bake the woman so many casseroles she wouldn't know what hit her, if that's what it took.

"I, ah…you don't need to do that. Seriously."

Becky shrugged. "Then come over for dinners. There's no need to be eating alone, especially in a house full of memories." She leaned forward and gave her old friend a quick hug. "Whatever happened in the past, I've missed you, Nikki, and I want my friend back."

She waited for Nikki to say something, anything, but she didn't. Once again, at the subject of their past, there was only silence.

She tried really hard to not let it bother her as she headed back down towards her vehicle, but it did.

It really, really did.

CHAPTER 7

~Nikki~

NIKKI POURED herself another cup of coffee and watched the sunrise out the window. The night before, she'd managed to get a lot more packed than she thought she would. Of course, after Becky's surprise visit, she'd been spooled up. And there really was no chance of doing anything else for the rest of the day besides pack. And, as it turned out, most of the night, because there was no way she could sleep. She was even able to quickly do up the flyers for the festival and send them off to Melissa.

The last thing she'd expected after Matt's surprise visit and subsequent discovery was for Becky to show up on her porch. She'd expected her old friend would be home with her husband, hearing all about the illegitimate child he hadn't known he had and the terrible person Nikki was for keeping it from all of them.

Nikki had definitely expected a visit from Becky, all right. She just hadn't expected the one she got. Clearly, Matt hadn't told her anything about Ryan. If he had, a very different Becky would have shown up. Of that, she had no doubt. But why hadn't he told his wife about Ryan? Why hadn't he asked her more questions? And if he had, would she have answered them?

She turned away from the window and sipped at her coffee. So many questions. And there really weren't any answers. Not any that she'd want to hear, anyway. There was no point dwelling on it. Matt knew about Ryan; she couldn't change that. And if she was forced to be honest with herself, she wasn't sure whether she wanted to. Keeping the secret for ten years had been exhausting. Clearly, it had taken a toll on her mother as well. She didn't want to admit it, even to herself, but ever since Matt's visit the day before, a weight had definitely been lifted.

The sound of footsteps on the floor above reminded her that there was still someone who didn't know the truth. She'd have to tell Ryan about his dad. Especially because it was clear he already suspected something. Ryan was a smart kid. She couldn't hide forever.

"Hey, Mom."

She turned and her mood instantly shifted when she saw her son, freshly showered and dressed for the day, standing in front of her.

"Good morning," she said, moving to kiss him on the head. He dodged the kiss, and she pretended not to be bothered by it. "What's gotten into you this morning?"

She watched while Ryan moved to the cupboard and pulled out a coffee cup. "What do you mean?"

"I mean," she said slowly, not taking her eyes off him. "It's not like you to shower and get dressed without a little nagging. What's up?"

He took the pot and poured himself a cup of coffee and although Nikki's eyes widened in surprise, she still didn't say anything.

"I thought I'd help out a bit more today," he said and raised the cup to his lips. Nikki watched and waited. "Like I said, I'm not a kid anymore."

"No," she said. "You're not."

Ryan took a sip of the coffee and Nikki forced herself not to laugh when his face wrinkled up in response. She raised her own mug to hide her smile.

"How can you drink that stuff?" Ryan asked when he recovered. "It's terrible."

"You get used to it." Nikki moved to the refrigerator, pulled out the jug of orange juice and poured him a glass. He took it readily and gulped it down. "Why did you want to drink coffee anyway?"

Ryan wiped his face with the sleeve of his shirt and Nikki forced herself not to say anything about it. "I wanted to show you that I'm not a kid anymore. I'm ten now. That's practically a teenager and a teenager is practically grown up."

Nikki raised her eyebrows. "You think so, do you?"

"Mom. I'm serious." He was trying so hard to make his point, Nikki relented.

"Okay," she said. "I know you're growing up. But you're not grown up yet. So lay off the coffee, okay?"

"Not a problem."

She grabbed him a bowl and poured him some cereal before sitting across from him at the table. A feeling of nostalgia washed over her as she remembered so many similar mornings where she'd sat with her own mother, just the way they were.

"Are you sad?" Ryan asked through a mouth full of cereal.

Nikki wiped her face and the tears she hadn't meant to cry. "I was just thinking of Grandma," she said. "But I'm okay now."

"Are we going to her funeral? Declan, in my class, he went to his grandpa's funeral last year. He said lots of people cried and told stories about his grandpa. And they played songs and stuff. Are they going to do that for Grandma?"

"They are."

"And we're gonna go?"

"I don't know, Ryan. I think…" Her voice drifted off as she assessed her son. Her mother had wanted a funeral. Levi told her as much. But there was no way they could go, even if Levi did insist on going through with it. Everyone would see Ryan. They'd know. He'd know. Panic pricked at the back of her neck and she squeezed her mug a little tighter.

But Matt already knew. He knew.

"Mom?" Ryan dropped his spoon with a clatter in the bowl.

Nikki looked up with a start.

"So are we going?"

Nikki let out a breath. "Would you like that?" she asked. "Or would it make you sad?"

He looked down into his bowl. "I'm sad anyway." His small voice cracked. Nikki's heart broke a bit more. "But I think we should go. Grandma would want us to go."

He was right. There was nothing her mother would have wanted more than for Nikki to be in Halfway with her son. After everything, it was the least she could do for her mom. She nodded.

"You're right. She would have wanted it very much."

"So we'll go?"

"We'll go." Nikki forced a smile she didn't feel. She'd work out the details later. She'd have to.

###

SHE DIDN'T LIKE the idea of taking Ryan out of the house and into town. Despite what they may have decided on, she still wasn't ready to introduce him to the general population of Halfway. The funeral was still days away and surely Matt would have said something to Becky by then.

She couldn't be the one to tell her about Ryan. Especially not after hearing that they weren't able to have children of their own. When Becky had shared that with her the day before, it was all Nikki could do to continue sitting there on the porch with her. Becky wanted to forgive her for running away from their friendship. But how could she sit there and pretend she hadn't betrayed her in the worst way possible, all the while knowing that she had the one thing her friend would never have: Matt's child?

It was unthinkable. And she hated herself more the longer she stayed in the small town. The day after the funeral, they'd be gone. Nikki looked in the rearview mirror at her son.

But for now, she had details to take care of and she couldn't leave Ryan in a strange house with no one to watch him. There was no getting around it. She had to risk it.

"Where's your tablet? I thought you were going to bring it."

"The battery was dead," Ryan said. "I can come in with you. I want to see."

"It's a funeral home, buddy. Not a toy store." She tried to keep her voice light. "I just need to drop Grandma's clothes off and then we'll go."

"I want to see."

"There's nothing to see."

"Mom, I'm not going to break anything."

"I know. It'll just be faster if I run in, okay?"

"I'm not slow."

"Ryan," she snapped. "That's enough. Just wait in the car, okay?" They'd pulled up to Levi's and she put the car in park before looking in the mirror again. Ryan was biting his lip, trying not to cry.

She sighed. Just because she was losing control of everything did not mean she had to lose it on him. "Come on," she said with a sigh. "Let's go."

By the time Nikki grabbed her mother's clothes out of the

back, Ryan was already waiting on the sidewalk, with a smile on his face.

"It's really not that exciting," she mumbled as she led the way up the walk.

She pushed the door open, and the gentle ring of a bell announced their arrival. Levi operated his funeral home out of an old historical house on Main Street. He had a small apartment on the upper floor where he lived, and she could hear him shuffling around above her.

"I'll be right there," he called.

"Don't touch anything," Nikki whispered to Ryan, who was already moving around the room, looking at the few display coffins and silk flower arrangements.

She didn't have time to say anything else, because Levi appeared in the doorway.

"Nikki Landon. Look at you." He held out his arms. She put the package she was holding down on a nearby table and accepted his embrace. It felt good to be hugged by someone she'd known her whole life and Nikki almost let herself give in to her grief.

"Levi," she said when she stepped back. "You look the same as always. You haven't changed a bit."

"Neither have you," he said in his familiar rumbling voice. "You're still as beautiful as the last time I saw you."

Nikki blushed. "Levi, you old flirt. I'm ten years older and it shows."

"You're still a looker," he said. "Just like your mama was."

At the mention of her mother, Levi's eyes welled up with tears, but he blinked them away before she could say anything. A noise from the corner of the room caught their attention, and Nikki whipped around to see Ryan trying to catch a flower display he'd knocked over.

"Oh, Ryan." She darted over and grabbed the vase before it could crash to the ground. "I told you to be careful."

"No trouble," Levi said, coming up behind them. "And who's this?"

Nikki straightened the vase and stood behind Ryan. It was the moment she'd dreaded since returning to Halfway. But there was no other option. She took a deep breath. "Levi, this is my son, Ryan."

Like a little man, Ryan shot his hand out and said, "It's nice to meet you, sir."

Nikki smiled and if the situation would have been any different, she would have been able to appreciate her son's impeccable manners.

Levi shook Ryan's hand, and Nikki watched the old man's face transform as he looked first to the little boy and then to Nikki. And back. "It's nice to meet you," he said to Ryan. To Nikki, he added, "Your mother didn't say anything about a grandson."

Nikki saw the hurt on his face and she immediately regretted introducing Ryan to him in such a way. Levi and her mother were friends. Hadn't Becky said she thought he had a crush on her mom? Of course he'd be hurt if he discovered the woman he cared about had kept such a secret from him. How could she be so careless?

"Ryan, do you see those cards over there?" Nikki pointed to a shelf on the other side of the room. "Could you go pick out a design that we can use for Grandma's program?"

He nodded and, happy to have a task, headed off to take care of it. As soon as he was out of earshot, Nikki turned to Levi and whispered, "It's not that she didn't want to tell you. It's my fault."

His face was muddled with confusion.

"I asked her not to say anything to anyone in town about Ryan," Nikki tried to explain. "As you know, this is the first time we've been to visit. And, well, I just didn't want anyone to know my business, I guess."

"You didn't want your friends to know you had a son?" Levi pulled on his beard and stared intently at Ryan.

"It's complicated, Levi. I can't really get into it right now."

"Mom," Ryan called. He turned in their direction, holding up a card. "I found one I think Grandma would've liked. It has lilacs on it. She liked those the best."

Next to her, she heard Levi take a sharp breath. And she knew he'd seen the resemblance and figured it out. There was no way it could be missed.

Emotion flooded Nikki, but it wasn't her who answered Ryan.

"Yes," Levi said. He walked to Ryan and squatted so he was at the same height. "You're absolutely right. Lilacs were her favorite. I think it's a perfect choice."

When he stood and returned to Nikki, the card in his hand, he didn't say any more about the subject. He simply nodded, and she knew he understood, even if he didn't agree.

###

When they got back in the car, Nikki wasn't ready to go back to the house. Nothing but memories and boxes were waiting for her there. Feeling bolder after their visit with Levi, she spun around in her seat. "What do you think about stopping by Grounds and getting one of those hot chocolates I told you about?"

"Can we?" Ryan's face lit up the way she knew it would. He wasn't going to turn down a treat. "Really?"

"Really."

She faced front and turned the key in the ignition. There was no point hiding. Matt knew the truth, and now so did Levi. It was only a matter of time before word got out. And when it did, she would handle it. But she was done hiding.

Nikki steered the car down the icy streets towards Grounds

and pulled up in front. Ryan bounded from the car before she had a chance to grab her purse and get her door open. She laughed as she joined him on the sidewalk.

"If I didn't know better, I'd think you'd never had a hot chocolate before the way you're acting."

Ryan rubbed his stomach. "I love it."

"Are you sure you don't want a coffee?" she teased.

He blushed, one of the few traits he'd inherited from her, and shook his head. "I think I'm done with coffee for a while."

"Good." Nikki put her hand on his shoulder, noting how tall he was getting and spun him around to face the shop. But instead of taking a step down the sidewalk, she froze.

"Matt."

"Nikki." He nodded at her but she didn't miss the way his gaze lingered on her son. Their son. "Ryan? It's...it's nice to see you both." He stumbled over his words and looked up at her again. His eyes were full of emotions Nikki couldn't decipher, and it pained her to realize there once was a time when she would have known exactly what he was feeling.

"We were just about to get a hot chocolate," Nikki said.

"Do you want one?" Ryan blurted out the question and both Nikki and Matt stared at him.

"No," Matt said after a moment, and then added, "Not this time."

"Next time then," Ryan said confidently. He looked up at Nikki. "Ready?"

Nikki's head spun with the poignancy of the situation. But she needed to be strong. There wasn't another choice. She reached into her purse and handed Ryan a twenty. "You know what, buddy? Since you're so grown up and all, why don't you go place the order? I need to talk to Matt about something."

He didn't need to be asked twice. Ryan, clearly pumped about the opportunity to show his maturity, grabbed the money and headed into the store. Before he slipped inside, he turned and said, "Maybe we'll see you again, Matt?"

"Yeah." Matt nodded. "I think so."

Satisfied, Ryan went inside to complete his task.

"What are you thinking?" Matt asked the moment he was gone. "You can't bring him here."

As if she'd been slapped, Nikki stepped back. Whatever she'd expected, she didn't expect that response from Matt. "Bring him to Grounds? Are you kidding me?"

"Nikki, people will see him. And he looks...he looks...well, he looks just like me," he finished. "What are people going to think?"

Anger flared through her. For all the mistakes she'd made, her first priority had always been Ryan. And that hadn't changed. She stepped up and straightened her shoulders. "They're going to think the same thing you did when you saw him. That he's your son."

"But, I—"

"And they'll be right," Nikki said, not backing down. "He's your son, Matt. And I'm sorry I didn't tell you. I have made mistakes. I'll admit that. And we can talk about that. You deserve that from me, I know that. But this isn't the time or the place for that conversation."

"Nikki." He scrubbed a hand over his face. "This is crazy. I don't know what to do here."

"You were right when you said people were going to notice the resemblance, Matt. And I'm not going to hide him. He's my child and I'm done with secrets." She pulled her purse higher on her shoulder. "So may I suggest that before your wife makes the same connection, you be the one to tell her that you have a child? He's ten and his name is Ryan."

CHAPTER 8

~Becky~

BECKY'S FINGERS tapped on the counter as she checked off things from the new to-do list Norma had given her at the hospital earlier. Instead of the praise over what she had completed, she'd had a long list of items thrust at her and then given a stern lecture on how certain things needed to be done.

Like normal. Why would she have expected anything different?

Just once, she'd like her mother to tell her what a great job she was doing. Because she was. Everything was on schedule, no issues had popped up last minute, and everyone was ready for this festival to begin. It helped that everyone knew Norma was in the hospital so they all stepped up to ensure things ran smoothly, just like a small town would. That was one of the benefits of living in a town like Halfway.

She tried really hard not to look at the clock or her phone. A plate of cold spaghetti and meatballs sat at the kitchen table for

Matt for whenever he decided to come home. Last night, she'd gone to bed alone and she'd woken up the same way. She had a feeling Matt had slept in the spare bedroom rather than wake her up when he climbed into bed. He often did that when he was out in the fields late and it was something she'd just gotten used to over the years.

What she wasn't used to was his silence. Sure, he might have slept in a separate bed, but he always left her a note on the counter for her to find or sent her texts throughout the day. She'd sent him a few but when he didn't respond by noon, she figured he was busy.

She didn't figure that anymore. Something was wrong. She knew it.

Sure, they were behind on some bills, but they weren't the only ones. And yes, having her mom in the hospital added a bit more stress than normal at this time of the year, but again, that was something they could deal with. Or normally would deal with together.

They were known as a power couple in town. The high school sweethearts. The ones who would make it through, no matter what. A lot of their friends were either divorced or separated or just trying to find a way to make it through another day while raising a family.

But not her and Matt. Their love was just as strong as it had been when they started dating in high school. Stronger even. They'd weathered their own storms but made it through and Becky had no doubt no matter what came their way, they'd be just fine.

Just fine. So why did the thought feel like a heavy burden?

A light outside caught her attention and she turned to watch the headlights from Matt's truck illuminate the driveway.

The tight vice-like grip around her heart disappeared now that he was home. She inhaled, breathing in the crisp air and then slowly exhaled.

On her way to the door, she flipped the switch on the coffee maker. By the time he got in and was settled, the coffee would be brewed. She looked forward to a quiet night with him; it had been a while since they'd had one and it would probably be their last night with both of them at home until Christmas Day.

She stood and watched as he crossed the driveway towards her. His arms were laced behind him so she held the screen open for him and tried to peek over his shoulder to see what he was carrying.

"I'm sorry," he said as he held a bouquet of flowers in one hand and a bottle of red wine in his other.

Becky searched his gaze. He had nothing to apologize for, but there was something in his look, something that had her swallow back her words. She nodded as she took the bouquet and headed towards the kitchen.

She busied herself with finding a vase and filling it with the flowers. She added a teaspoon of sugar to the water before cutting the stems on an angle and placing them inside the vase. Matt sat at the counter and watched her. It was a bit disconcerting.

"Is everything almost ready?" She figured his day must have been spent getting the tree lot organized.

"Just about. The fences went up today and Bob is organizing a schedule. We'll wait as long as we can before we start cutting down the trees." The trees they sent down South or up to Canada were always cut earlier in the season, but the local trees were saved for last. "What smells so good?" Matt rubbed at his face.

Becky poured coffee into his mug and set it in front of him. "Cinnamon buns. I wasn't sure if you'd be hungry or not." She pointed towards the plate of spaghetti on the table.

"I totally forgot to send you a text. Bob asked me to join him at the pub for a burger and we went over the schedule. I'm sorry."

"I'd almost think you were trying to avoid me." She stared at him, hands on her hips. "You're not, are you?"

When Matt didn't respond, Becky's hand fisted together before she went to grab the dinner she'd left for Matt and cover it with wrap before placing it in the fridge.

"I'm going to go have a shower," Matt muttered before he drank the last of his coffee and stood.

"Excuse me?"

"I won't be long."

Becky shook her head. "That's not the point. I haven't seen you for two days but the minute you're home, it seems like you're trying to find ways to not be around me."

Matt pulled her into his arms and held her tightly. "I'm not avoiding you, I promise."

She pushed him away as she wrinkled her nose. "Then go have your shower. There's nothing worse than sharing my cinnamon buns with a stinky man." She attempted to smile while he gave her a searching look before he placed a small kiss on her cheek and left the room.

Becky puttered around the kitchen, tidying it up while responding to emails on her phone regarding the festival. There were so many last-minute things to consider, like making sure the bulbs in the lights that strung around the tree all worked. She'd have to dig them out of her mother's garage and go through them tomorrow.

She tried really hard not to think about the fact her husband was obviously avoiding her. In the past, anytime he stayed in town for something to eat, he always asked her to join him. This was the first, that she knew of, where she hadn't been welcomed. It hurt.

Why was her husband pulling away so suddenly? Everything had been fine between them until yesterday.

Just as she heard the water turn off from the upstairs bathroom, the oven dinged to let her know her pastry was done. She pulled the tray out of the oven and set it on a wire rack to cool before she headed into her office for her camera. She liked to take various images of her baked goods, sometimes even taking pictures of the whole process. But tonight she just wanted an image of the golden brown crust before the cream cheese icing went on to post on the various social websites she visited.

She listened for the thud of Matt's footsteps on the stairs before she headed into the kitchen with her camera. Her grip was tight and she fumbled with the lens as she attempted to find the right light for the shot. Her nerves were on end and there was a heaviness to the room when he sat at the table.

She went to reach for her coffee cup but bypassed it when she caught sight of the bottle of wine he'd brought home. She poured some through an aerator into her glass and while it sat, she prepared two cinnamon buns. She needed to keep her hands busy while Matt just sat there, watching her with a look on his face like his world was about to end.

"Mom will be out of the hospital soon," she said to break the silence.

"Is she coming to stay with us, like we planned, or back to her place?"

"Her place. You know how she is." Stubborn, that's what her mother was. "She's already got home care set up to help her, too." Which was ridiculous because Becky planned to be there as much as she could to help out.

"Have you talked to Nikki?" Matt blurted.

"Not since yesterday. I stopped by to chat and talk about the festival. I thought…well, I thought we'd be able to pick up where we left off, but I guess she just needs a bit more time."

"Did you…did you meet her son?"

Becky had the wine glass raised to her lips and paused. *Her son?*

"No…" But it would explain why she'd been so focused on looking through the window and why she'd never been invited into the house. *A son?* Nikki had a child. The thought crushed her. "Did you?"

Matt nodded.

"How old is he? A baby?" Her voice squeaked.

He shook his head.

"I can't believe she has a child. She never said anything. Mom never said anything. How could I not know this?"

"Maybe your mom didn't know."

Becky snorted. "As if. Mom knows everything. And it's not like Marie would have kept this from her. They were practically sisters."

"She might have had her reasons for keeping the secret."

"Why didn't she say anything to me? We even talked about having kids," Becky muttered to herself as she took a sip of her wine.

"How old is he? What's his name? How did you meet him?" Becky barraged her husband with questions. It wasn't fair that he knew the answers before she did. Nikki had been her best friend. Not his. Well, technically they had all been close, but still, it wasn't fair.

"Ryan. His name is Ryan. And I," he cleared his throat, "I don't think Nikki meant for me to see him."

"When? Today?"

Matt had a telltale sign when he was upset. A little spot in his cheek became indented whenever he ground his teeth together.

"The other day."

Her brow rose. "You've known she had a child for days now and you're just telling me?"

Why? It didn't make sense. Was that why she'd canceled dinner for the other night? Because she hadn't wanted them to meet her son? Why the secrecy?

"How old is he?"

"Ten."

Her best friend had a ten-year-old son that no one in Halfway had known about.

"Oh my…" That's when it hit her. "Someone from here must

be the father. That's why she left like she did and has never come back."

At the stricken look on Matt's face, she knew she'd guessed correctly. "Do you know who?"

Becky tried to think back. She'd gone to prom with Parker and then left shortly after.

"I can't believe she would have kept something like that a secret from me." For years, she'd wondered why Nikki had run off the way she did. She couldn't have imagined what Nikki had gone through, finding out she was pregnant at such a young age. But why did she leave? Hadn't she known that she would have been supported, that Becky would have stood by her, no matter what?

And why keep it a secret for ten years? Did the father even know? Was that why she never came back, because she didn't want him to know? Or did she tell him and he didn't want the baby? Was that why she'd left?

"Whatever you're thinking, stop." Matt reached for her hand and grabbed hold. "There's something you need to know."

"Like what?" She stilled and she could feel her heart slow down until the sound of it thudded in her ears.

"I love you—you know that, right?" Matt tightened his grip.

"Of course. I love you, too."

"It's always been you. There's never been anyone else in my life. Never. From the moment I first saw you, I knew you would be mine."

Becky nodded. She knew that. She'd always known that. There had never been anyone else for her either. They'd started out as best friends and remained that way throughout everything. Matt had been her first love, her first kiss, and her first lover.

Just as she'd been his.

"But there was that time when we'd broken up, just before finals and school ended. Remember?"

Remember? How could she forget? That had been the worst month of her life. Matt's dad had his first stroke and instead of letting Becky be there for him, Matt had pushed her away. He'd told her that his life would be forever tethered to Halfway and Becky deserved more, deserved to see the world, like she'd always dreamed about. So he broke up with her. She'd been heartbroken and locked herself in her room for weeks. She wouldn't even see Nikki, not at first. But then when she'd been ready and realized that she needed to fight for her and Matt, Nikki hadn't wanted to see her. She'd become distant for a while. Until…until she and Matt had gotten back together.

"I made a mistake. It was one time and I'll forever regret it, but…"

Becky's knees buckled from beneath her and she gripped the counter for support. She'd wrenched her hand out from under her husband's, not wanting his touch.

The room spun around her and she barely heard the words Matt said. She saw his mouth move, but everything was garbled.

It didn't matter, though. "Don't say it," she pleaded. Her voice had dulled and when he reached out towards her, she stepped back. "No, don't. Please, just don't."

He was the father. Matt. Her husband.

"Becky…" His voice broke and she saw the torment in his eyes but it didn't matter to her, not right then.

"No. I don't want to hear it. Please…" *If he said the words, then they'd be true, right?* Maybe she was exaggerating. Maybe it wasn't this at all—maybe…

"How? How could you and not tell me? Why wouldn't you tell me? How could you lie about something like this?" Her stomach twisted at the thought of Matt and Nikki together, all those years ago. How could she not have known?

"I didn't know. Please, I need you to believe me." His voice cracked. "I didn't know."

Becky's eyes stung. "Didn't know? How could you not? You

slept with her!" Her voice rose until she was yelling. "You slept with my best friend and never told me. How could you?"

"I'm sorry," he whispered. "I'm so sorry."

She backed away from him, not wanting to be near him, not wanting to see his face, to see the emotions written so plainly for anyone to see.

She wasn't sure what hurt her the most: the fact that he'd betrayed her or that the realization that he was a father of a child who wasn't hers.

CHAPTER 9

❄

~*Nikki*~

After more or less announcing Ryan to the town of Halfway, Nikki expected to feel exhausted or anxious. Instead, she returned to her childhood home feeling better than she had in a long time. As if a weight had been lifted off her, a very heavy weight of lies and secrets. It was freeing that Matt finally knew the truth. But at the same time, it was terrifying.

Clearly Matt hadn't told Becky about her son. *Their son*, she mentally corrected herself. But he would soon. She was sure of that now. And when he did, Nikki had a feeling she wasn't going to be feeling such a sense of relief anymore. So for the moment, she was going to enjoy the peace.

When they got back to the house, Ryan wanted to explore in the attic, and he promised that he would even pack up a few boxes if Nikki let him play with any of her old toys that they found. There was no way she could say no to that offer, so they each grabbed a stack of flattened boxes and made their way upstairs.

Growing up in an old-style home with a traditional attic had been fun for her as a child, and it was nice to see that Ryan enjoyed it the same way she once had, hiding in the nooks and crannies, digging through her mother's trunks of old clothes, and discovering all kinds of unique treasures.

As an adult, especially one who was trying to pack up an entire house full of memories and a lifetime full of stuff, Nikki wasn't enjoying the attic as much as she once had. The space was packed with boxes and trunks of God knows what. "What are we going to do with all this stuff?" she asked Ryan, who had his head stuck into a chest and was pulling out trophies.

"It's cool," was his mumbled response. "I didn't know you were a track star." He emerged from the chest holding one of the larger trophies she'd earned.

"I would hardly say I was a star." She crossed the space and took the trophy from his hand, running her fingers over the engraved 1st Place State Meet lettering. "But I guess I did win a few races. I ran cross country. Sprinting wasn't my thing."

Ryan wrinkled up his nose. "I hate running."

"You get that from your father," she said, remembering how Matt would avoid any type of long-distance running.

"My dad?"

Nikki realized her mistake a moment too late. She squeezed her eyes shut and swallowed hard.

"What else did my dad hate?" Ryan asked.

She didn't like to lie to her son, but she also knew she couldn't tell him the truth. Not yet. It was one thing for Matt to know the truth and even for some of the other townspeople to figure it out on their own. But she couldn't tell Ryan. Not until she knew how Matt and Becky were going to handle the situation. She'd tell him. Just not yet. So she resorted to her usual tactic of avoidance.

"Why don't we see what else is in here?"

Ryan opened his mouth to say something, but thankfully he didn't push the issue. He usually didn't. It was almost as if he could sense that it was a sore subject for his mother. He was a smart kid and a sensitive one, too. She needed to handle the situation carefully. Especially considering she'd already made such a mess of it.

"Look at this," Nikki said, pulling out a large book. "This is my old yearbook. I can show you a picture of me earning that trophy."

Ryan seemed momentarily satisfied with that, and slid closer so he could look at the book.

Nikki knew exactly where to turn and she flipped the pages until she found the shot she was looking for. It was her, crossing the finish line at the state track meet. Her hands were in the air, a huge smile on her face—complete bliss. The girl in that picture had no idea how her life would change in only a few short weeks. For that Nikki, everything was right in the world.

Ryan pointed at the picture and laughed. "Did you really wear socks like that?"

"What's wrong with those socks?"

"They're huge, Mom."

They were huge. Nikki turned her attention back to the picture, although she didn't need to in order to remember those socks. Becky had given them to her as a good luck gift. The black-and-white picture didn't show it, but they were rainbow striped, and so bright that Nikki was sure she probably blinded half the competition.

"My best friend gave me those," she told Ryan. "They were for good luck."

"For luck?" Ryan gave his mom a doubtful look.

"They worked, didn't they? I have the trophy to prove it."

"True." Ryan nodded slowly and took the book from her hands. "Is there a picture of your friend? Can I see her?"

There was no harm in showing her son pictures, especially because she had a feeling that in some way, although she didn't know how yet, Becky was going to be a part of his life. Nikki flipped through the pages until she got to the senior class. "That's Becky." She pointed to a portrait that, even though it was in black and white, showcased a stunning girl. Becky was one of the prettiest girls in their class, if not the whole town. Every boy wanted to date her and she could have had her pick.

But she didn't pick any boy, Nikki reminded herself. She'd picked Matt.

"You know what, Ryan? I think those socks are probably in a box over there. I think I saw one labeled 'Nikki's Things.' Why don't you go dig through there?" Ryan didn't need to be asked twice. He jumped up and eagerly started digging through boxes.

Nikki returned her attention to the yearbook and flipped the page until she saw the picture of the boy she'd loved back then. Matt Jennings. She'd loved him first. And maybe things would have been different, too, if she'd spoken up. But she hadn't.

There'd been a time when Matt loved her, too. Or at least she thought he had. There'd been flirting, phone calls, and even a date that ended with a kiss. Nikki couldn't remember being so happy. But then Becky announced that she liked Matt. To be fair, Nikki didn't tell Becky how she felt. She'd kept it quiet, enjoying the secret she had.

But Becky was a force of nature, and whenever she wanted something, she went after it. Once she set her sights on Matt, Nikki knew there was no point. Her best friend always got the guy. It was a fact.

So she'd stepped aside.

Except that one night.

Her mom was out with Norma at some sort of charity meeting and she'd been catching up on homework when the doorbell rang. Matt was standing on the porch, looking lost and utterly broken. Of course she'd invited him in and they'd talked.

A lot. He'd just come from Becky's house, where he'd broken up with her, and when Matt kissed her, Nikki knew she should have pushed him away. She knew in her heart he wasn't kissing her for anything more than comfort and it was wrong. But she'd let her heart lead the way and soon the kisses turned into more and—

"Mom! I found them."

Nikki closed the yearbook and looked up to see that in fact, Ryan had indeed found the socks.

She laughed and went to join him across the room. "I can't believe she kept them." She shook her head. "Well, actually I can. Mom kept everything."

"You should wear them, Mom. They're awesome."

"Weren't you making fun of them a minute ago?"

"That's before I knew they were lucky. Can I wear them?"

Nikki laughed. "You can have them."

"Awesome." Ryan tugged the socks on over his jeans.

Ryan got up and danced around the small space, causing Nikki to break into laughter. The type of deep belly laughing that took her breath away in a very good, long overdue way. When she was finally able to pull herself together, she wiped her eyes with the corner of her t-shirt, and asked, "What do you need luck for, anyway?"

Ryan dropped to his knees in front of the box he'd just been digging through. "What don't I need luck for? Maybe I'll find something really cool in here. Do you have anything that was my dad's?"

Nikki froze. She'd only ever touched on the truth with Ryan. She'd told him that she'd gone to high school with his dad and then they'd lost touch. It was partially true. And Ryan had always been too young to want to know too much more. She'd spent years deflecting his questions and putting him off, until he'd stopped asking much. At least until they'd come back to Halfway. She wasn't stupid, and she knew she'd made some huge mistakes where Ryan was concerned. And he was old enough to know the truth. That much she had decided on.

It was just a matter of when to tell him.

She blinked hard and watched as Ryan started unearthing random items from the box. Her mother truly had kept everything. "I don't know what you'll find in there," she answered honestly.

"Do you think my dad knows you're back in town, Mom?"

She took a deep breath and nodded slowly. "I think he probably knows."

"Will he want to come and meet me? I think I'd like to meet him."

Her chest ached, thinking of the mess she'd made. "I think he might, buddy. But we need to remember why we're here, okay?"

The pain intensified when she saw the disappointment on his face. He was just a kid who expected the best from everyone, and so far his mother had been the one to let him down. "Come here, Ryan."

Ryan shuffled over on his knees and fell into his mom's arms, where she held him and stroked his hair. He was getting so big—it wasn't often that he let her get a cuddle in, and she relished those moments. "Why don't we see if we can find a snack downstairs? I think that's enough organizing for right now." She looked around the space, and the piles they'd made. There was still so much to do, she wasn't sure how she'd ever get it finished. But that didn't matter. Not right now.

Together they went downstairs and rummaged in the cupboards until she came up with a bag of cookies. Nikki watched Ryan dig into the treat and knew that food wasn't going to distract him for very long. She'd need to face the truth, sooner rather than later. Not for the first time, she found herself wishing her mother was still around so she could get some advice.

"I'll be in the living room, buddy, okay?"

Ryan looked up long enough to nod and Nikki moved through

the door, straight to the photo he'd put on the mantel of him with his grandma. She'd never pushed Nikki to tell the truth or come clean with anybody involved. In fact, she'd never said anything one way or the other about Nikki's choice. Sure, Nikki knew her opinion, or at least she'd thought she did. She ran her finger along the image of her mother. Maybe Nikki hadn't known how her mother really felt about her choices after all. She'd never asked.

It didn't matter, because now that Nikki wanted to know, and wanted her mother's advice, she couldn't get it. She was all alone.

A knock on the door startled her and she wiped at her face and the tear that had slipped from her eye. Without returning the photo to the mantel, she answered the door, looking through the glass as she turned the handle.

"Levi," she said as she opened the door wide. "What can I do for you? Did I forget something earlier? I thought I'd—"

"Oh, no, you brought everything." His smile was warm and Nikki had the overwhelming urge to hug him. "But you left before I could tell you that if you needed anything while you were here, you just have to ask."

"Thank you. That means a lot."

He stuffed his hands in his pockets awkwardly and shuffled from side to side. "I mean it, Nikki. I know there's a lot I don't know about, and your mother...well, I'm sure she had her reasons for keeping secrets, but—"

"Levi. That was my fault." Nikki stepped out onto the porch. "I asked her to keep the secret. It wasn't her choice. I'm sure she would have told you, but..."

He nodded, understanding, but Nikki could still see the lingering hurt there. "She meant a lot to me, your mother."

"I can see that." She smiled and handed him the photo she still held. "I think it would have made her very happy for you to see this."

She watched as he took the photo and just as she had earlier, ran his fingers along the outline of her mother's image. "She looks so happy here," he said after a moment.

"Ryan made her very happy. Nobody loved him the way she did. It was wrong of me to—"

"That's enough, now," Levi cut her off. "You had your reasons. And what's done is done. You can't look back anymore. There's nothing to be gained from that. Okay?"

She nodded.

"Can I use this photo at the service?"

Nikki didn't even hesitate when she answered. "Of course. I think she would like that very much."

"I think you're right, but...well, you're sure about it?"

She knew what he was asking. The old man was perceptive and it didn't take much to figure out the truth and what using the photo would mean. But it didn't matter.

She nodded. "I'm sure. It's time. It's way past time."

Levi smiled and tugged on his beard. "I know your mother would be very proud of you right now."

Tears sprang to her eyes and she sniffed them back as much as she could.

"But that's not the only reason I came here," Levi said, his voice shifting, becoming lighter. "I was going to go down and watch the ice carving. I don't know if you remember, but every year the McPherson brothers get their chainsaws out and try to out-do each other in preparation for the festival."

Nikki smiled with the memory. "I remember. I used to love watching that."

"Well, your mother liked it, too. It was actually something we always did together and I thought that maybe this year...well, maybe the boy would like to come with me."

Nikki's heart almost burst with appreciation and love for the man. She didn't even bother wiping her tears this time but instead threw her arms around a shocked Levi, and gave him a hug. After a moment, his arms wrapped around her and stroked the back of her head while she cried.

"Now, now," he mumbled. "Crying won't fix anything. But you go right ahead and get it out. Everything will be okay."

Nikki gave herself over to the tears and emotion, and wished she could believe him.

CHAPTER 10

~Becky~

WITH AUTOMATED MOTIONS, Becky prepared a lunch for Matt and filled up his thermos with coffee before he headed out back to mark more trees to be cut. The house was silent; barely a word had been spoken between the two of them since Matt's bombshell from last night. She couldn't look him in the eye, couldn't fathom his betrayal…couldn't handle her guilt, knowing someone else had given him a child when her own body wouldn't.

She wasn't sure whom she was madder at: Matt for betraying her with Nikki or Nikki for betraying their friendship by sleeping with Matt and then running away with his child.

Was she even mad at Matt? She wasn't sure whether her anger was even valid. He'd tried to explain that it had been a lapse in judgment, that it had happened while they'd broken up and that he'd instantly regretted it. Was it right of her to hold something that happened more than ten years ago over his head like that? Was it even fair to think she had the right to be angry about that?

All night, while she lay in their bed alone, she tried to remember how things had been back then, during their breakup. Nikki's actions now made sense, why she backed away from her. Had she been waiting all along for them to break up so she could swoop in and seduce her husband?

Just the thought made her blood boil.

How could she do that to her? They were supposed to have been best friends. Like sisters.

Her heart continued to splinter apart as she thought about it. She'd mourned the loss of her friend for too long. She'd been so naive in thinking they could start over, that they could pick up from where they'd left off.

There was no picking up the pieces of this shattered dream. Their friendship was over and it was time for Becky to grow up and realize it had been for a long, long time.

What did this boy, Ryan, look like? Did he look more like Matt or Nikki? Would she be able to tell right away he was Matt's child?

As she drove into town to visit her mother at the hospital, she was tempted to drive past Nikki's place, to see whether she could catch a glimpse of the boy. But she didn't.

How could Nikki have kept such a thing a secret?

After parking in front of the doors of the hospital, Becky leaned her head back against the seat. She needed to get her act together. She needed to push this out of her mind, for now, and focus on the festival, when all she wanted to do was cry on her mother's shoulder.

She could imagine what Norma would say. *Life doesn't always play favorites, so deal with it.* Well, she was tired of having to *deal with it*. With every miscarriage, she'd tried to *deal with it* and look where it left her—barren.

"Do you need help?" Uncle Dennis stood at her car door and

knocked on the window. Becky pasted a smile on her face and shook her head. Dennis opened the door for her and she gathered her purse and notebook before she took his offered hand and got out of her vehicle.

"What's up, lil' missy?"

She shook her head. She wasn't even sure how to handle this.

"Your mother's about to be released, from what I hear. Good thing, too. I think her nurses are due a vacation." He chuckled as he led her up the stairs and opened the door for her.

"What will she do when she gets old?" Becky placed a small kiss on her uncle's cheek.

"Your mother doesn't know what that word means. She'll outlive us all, with her crotchetiness."

She was able to keep her emotions in check until she stepped into her mother's room. Her mother sat there with an expectant look. The weariness that had hung over her was gone and the pale pallor that was in her face had transformed to an almost healthy color. Tears welled up in Becky's eyes and it was all she could do to not sob. She sank down in the chair beside her mom's bed and leaned forward, placing her head in her hands.

"What's wrong?" her mom asked.

Becky just shook her head, not trusting herself to speak.

"Did something happen? Is it Matt?"

Again, Becky shook her head but hearing the concern in her mother's voice seemed to bolster her, and she was able to sit back without letting the tears fall.

"Did you know Nikki had a child?" She stared up at the ceiling light and blinked. When Norma didn't respond, a stone settled in Becky's stomach and she felt ready to get sick. "You knew?"

Norma gave her head a tiny shake but then she nodded. "I knew. But not from Marie. I saw pictures one time, a few years ago, of Nikki with a little boy."

"And you never said anything?"

"Wasn't for me to say. Marie had her reasons, I'm sure, for keeping such a thing a secret." She rubbed her hands together.

Becky snorted. "Of course she did."

"Rebecca."

"No. You don't get to sound like that. It wasn't fair of Nikki or her mother to keep such a thing a secret."

"Is that why you're mad? Because Nikki kept it a secret from you?"

Becky shook her head. *If only her mother knew.*

"So you don't know his name or how old he is or even who the father is?"

Norma's lips thinned. "What do you think? Marie had her reasons. I knew she'd tell me if she needed to. I figured something had to have happened to make her bolt the way she did and never return." Norma sighed as she leaned back against her pillow. "Being a single mother, especially a teenage mother, had to have been hard. I never understood how she could cut herself off from everyone, especially you, like she did, but once I saw those photos, I figured she had her reasons."

Becky pushed herself up from her chair. The anger that bubbled beneath the surface of her heart boiled over listening to her mother stand up for Nikki.

"Her reasons? You want to know what her reasons were? Our sweet Nikki, the one everyone thought to be an angel, seduced my husband and ended up pregnant." She went to the window and leaned her hip against the wall, staring out into the park that was across the road. The same park where she had to start setting up for the festival later.

"What do you mean, seduced your husband?"

Becky whirled to stare at her mother. "Remember when Matt and I split up for that short period of time? Well, my best friend swooped in and tried to steal him from me."

"Oh, Becky," Norma sighed, "you guys were only dating back then. You can't be mad at her for that mistake."

Becky's brows rose. "I can't? Why can't I? She was my best friend, Mom. My"—her voice broke—"best friend." This time the tears did run down her cheeks.

Norma patted a spot on the bed beside her and Becky almost ran to it. She sat down and let her mother gather her in her arms. With her head on her mother's shoulder, Becky gave in to all the emotions that ran through her and cried.

After a few minutes, her mother pushed her away. "Is that what you're really upset about?"

Becky looked at her in confusion. Of course that was the reason.

"Being a mother has been a strong desire for you for a long time. I can't imagine how hard this must be for you, knowing someone else gave your husband something you've tried to do but can't." The sympathy in her mother's eyes softened her words. But not by much.

"I can still give him a child. I'll still be a mother, one day." She knew in her heart it was a moot point but she still needed to say it.

"Oh honey, you might think I haven't noticed, but I'm still your mother. I know the signs. I have my own angel babies, remember. But I think you're forgetting something."

"What?" She didn't want to think about her angels. Not now.

"You already are a mother."

Becky pushed herself up, away from her mother and shook her head.

"He's not my child. He's Matt's and Nikki's. He's theirs. Not mine."

"Rebecca Jennings, I raised you better than that. If he's Matt's child, then he's yours as well."

Becky wrapped her arms around her body. "But I...but he...oh my..." She sighed deep. She hadn't thought about that aspect. Well, to be honest, she hadn't wanted to. The idea had brushed her thoughts all night but she refused to think about it. That she was now a mother. Maybe not the kind of mother she had wanted to be, nor was Ryan the child she dreamed of…

"How does Matt feel about all this?"

Becky shrugged. "We haven't really talked about that." But they needed to. They would. They had no choice.

"What happens when Nikki leaves again?"

"Well…she can't. Can she?" At Norma's shrug, a tight fist grabbed Becky's heart. "She can't take Matt's child away from him, not now, not like this. He's ten years old, Mom. Ten. There's no way Matt's going to be willing to lose any more time with him than he already has."

Norma gave a deep nod. "Good. Good. So why don't you go find your husband and talk about this? I doubt you have much time left. Marie's funeral is in a few days. Levi's managed to convince that girl to stay for her own mother's funeral but I doubt she'll stick around long after. If you want to be part of that boy's life, you'd better do something about it now."

Renewed with a sense of purpose, one that she didn't have before, she grabbed her purse, gave her mother a quick kiss and hug, and then left the room.

"But don't forget to check all the lights first!" Her mother's voice followed her down the hallway.

###

W*e need to talk. I'm sorry I wasn't ready to last night.* Becky sent Matt a text. *Meet for hot chocolate? Heading to the park to go through the lights.*

Matt deserved a better apology, and she knew that. But she'd wait until they were face to face to give it to him. Last night she'd been selfish and nursed her wounded ego, not once considering what her husband must have been going through to realize he had a child he'd never known about.

She was still angry that he hadn't been faithful to her but if she were to be honest, it was a moot point now. It wasn't right of her to hold that indiscretion over his head, not after all these years. She'd never doubted him before and wouldn't let this creep up into their marriage to cause an issue.

As she made her way to the park carrying the Tupperware containers of lights, she knew they needed to be a strong unit in this, just like they'd always been in the past.

"There you are. Here, let me take those." Gus, from the hardware shop, grabbed the containers from her and hefted them in his arms. "Is this all there is? I thought Norma had more?"

Becky groaned. "She does. But I didn't have room. The rest are still in her garage."

"Give me the keys and I'll go grab them." Gus set the containers down by the pavilion in the middle of the park while Becky dug out her mother's house keys from her purse.

"If you take a look in her freezer, you might just find a container of jam with your name on it." Becky smiled her thanks as a grin crossed Gus's face as he took the keys, whistled to his son and headed towards his pick-up truck.

She was hoping she could sweet-talk someone into helping her with those lights. She couldn't believe how many containers her mother had stored in the rafters.

Her phone buzzed in her pocket. *Almost there. Need to set up area for trees. See you soon.*

Becky glanced around the park and smiled. This was probably her favorite time of the year, or one of them. Everything and anything that happened in this town was held in this park. In the summers, there were day camps, picnics, fruit markets, and sing-along nights. In the winter, there was the Tree Festival, and then Christmas markets, snowmen contests, snow fort contests and even ice sculpting...which reminded her...

"Oops, excuse me." She was nudged in the back and pushed forward. When she turned around, she found Nikki standing before her.

Everything Becky had thought of saying to Nikki last night vanished. She couldn't say anything. Her mouth opened and closed before she managed to say one word.

"No." It was whispered softly and she wasn't even sure Nikki heard her. "No," she said louder.

"I'm sorry?" Nikki stepped back with a confused look on her face. In her hands were stacks of paper.

"I won't excuse you. I've done it for too long. Ten years, to be exact."

She knew Nikki understood when her friend's eyes widened.

"You know," Becky gritted her teeth, "I waited for you to come home for years. Did your mom ever give you those letters I wrote in the beginning? Did she ever tell you how many times I dropped by to see if she'd heard from you?"

She'd be lying if she didn't admit to some sort of satisfaction when Nikki's gaze dropped to the snow-covered ground and her shoulders stooped.

"How could you?" She rolled her shoulders as tension knotted her muscles. She reminded herself to keep her voice low, to not bring unwanted attention to them. All it would take was one raised voice, one word of discord and all eyes would be on them.

"I'm sorry." Nikki sighed.

Becky snorted. *As if that would help in any way.* Her apology was ten years too late.

"Hey." Nikki straightened, her face hardening. "I know running away like I did wasn't the smartest move, but I can't change that now. You can be mad, but before you judge me, just remember, you don't know me anymore, Becky. You have no idea the sacrifices I had to make, how hard staying away has been. How hard all of it has been."

"You're right. I don't know you, and I obviously didn't know you back then either. I thought we were best friends, Nik. But best friends don't backstab one another, they don't sleep with the other's boyfriend and they sure as hell," by this time she'd started to yell and didn't care who heard, "don't keep the son of said friend's husband a secret."

She watched as a change came over the woman in front of her. Her stance relaxed and she even had the audacity to smile. *To smile?* That angered Becky more than anything.

"You're right. You obviously didn't know me. Because if you had, you would have known that I loved Matt even before you knew his name. You also would have known that I would have done anything for you and in fact did, when I stepped aside when you decided you liked him."

What?

"Since when did you like Matt?" Becky couldn't believe what she was hearing.

"Funny, how that's what you focus on. It doesn't matter, does it? You married him. You are the one he loves. I've grown up, moved on and realized he wasn't worth whatever feelings I'd had for him."

Becky bristled at that. She stepped forward until she invaded Nikki's personal space.

"Not worth it? He wasn't the one who ran away. He," she jabbed her finger into the down of Nikki's coat, "wasn't the one who kept his child away from him."

"No, he wasn't," she said softly. "That was me. All me."

All of Becky's anger dissipated at Nikki's admission. She had expected more...more excuses, more apologies, but not this. She stepped back and struggled to get her bearings. She glanced around the park and noticed how everyone had literally stopped what they were doing and had edged closer.

"Here are some copies of the flyers I made up. I figured you'd want to see them. I sent them to Melissa, too, but I made a few variations. I wasn't sure what you wanted."

Wordlessly, Becky took the stack of papers from Nikki's hands and watched as the person she once called her best friend turned and started to walk away from her.

"Nik?" she called out. "Nikki?"

Nikki stopped but didn't turn. Becky took a few steps towards her. "Listen, I'm sorry. I…Matt just told me, and I…"

Nikki then turned. "No need to apologize. Trust me."

Becky blushed. "But I do." She couldn't believe how upset she'd gotten. That wasn't like her. "And apparently for more than I realized."

Nikki just watched her, waiting.

"We need to talk. About your son. About Ryan. All of us—you, me, and Matt. And I'd like to meet him. Your son—"

"Our son." Matt appeared at her side and wrapped his arm around her waist. "Our son. We'd like to meet him and be introduced to him, properly, this time."

Becky watched as Nikki's face blanched at his words and was thankful that Matt had said what she couldn't say.

CHAPTER 11

~Nikki~

Meet Ryan? They wanted to meet Ryan? Nikki shook her head, but she couldn't be sure who she was shaking it at.

Of course, she'd known it was a possibility. It was more than a possibility and she'd always known it, even if she'd denied it to herself. Matt and Becky were good people; of course they were going to want to know their son.

But he wasn't their son. He was hers.

Ryan was hers.

She looked at them both in turn. Matt looked exhausted. His handsome features were clouded with an obvious lack of sleep, making him look a lot older than his years. But it was Becky's face that made her heart clench. She'd have to be blind not to see the hurt in her eyes. The pain that was all over her face. It may have been years since Nikki had called her best friend, but she still hurt with her. And she knew she'd deeply wounded her friend. Which is exactly what she'd been trying to avoid.

"Yes, Nikki," Becky said, breaking through her fog. "We want to meet him."

"He's not here," she said automatically.

Matt glanced around. "Where would he be? He's only ten, right?"

Her hackles went up. "I didn't leave him alone, if that's what you're implying. He's with—" She stopped herself. If she told them where Ryan was or who he was with, there'd be nothing stopping them from finding him on their own and she couldn't let that happen. Not before she could talk to him.

"Well," Becky said. "Where is he, Nikki? We want to meet him. He's our son."

Her words triggered something inside Nikki. "No," she said, and then pulling herself up and taking a deep breath, she said it again. Stronger this time. "No."

Becky took a step back and Matt caught her, wrapping a protective arm around her. Just like he used to. Hadn't it always eaten Nikki up to see the way he took care of her and worshipped the very ground Becky walked on, while she stood by, the third wheel best friend? When it was her heart that broke every time she saw the love between them. It could have been her. It should have been her.

No. She shook her head again. She hadn't felt that way in years. And despite everything, she didn't feel that way now. But she still wasn't going to stand by and let them take what was hers.

"Nikki, you're—"

"No," she said again, cutting Matt off. "He's not your son. He's mine."

"Nikki," Matt tried again. "You said…I mean, he's obviously mine."

Next to him, Becky seemed to sink into herself at his words. So he hadn't told her that Ryan was a spitting image of him, then.

"That doesn't make him your son," she said. "Not more than blood. It doesn't work that way."

"And whose fault is that?" Becky said, clearly regaining some of the anger she'd had earlier. "You kept him from us. You ran and hid like—"

"Like what?" Nikki challenged her. She'd always backed down to her best friend. Always given in to whatever Becky wanted, whatever it was Becky needed. That was before. She had more important things to worry about now.

Becky narrowed her eyes at her. "Like a coward," she finished.

The word hit her like a slap and fury burned through her. She took a step up to Becky, the first time she'd ever stood up to her, and spoke through clenched teeth. "A coward? Is that what you think I am?" She didn't give Becky a chance to answer. "Did you stop for one moment to think about why I left? Why, at barely eighteen years old, I might think it was a good idea to leave everything and everyone I knew to raise a baby by myself? Did you stop to think about it?"

Becky didn't answer, but her strong eyes didn't leave Nikki's.

"I did it for you," Nikki said, her voice softer now. "I did everything for you. I never told you how I felt about Matt because I knew it would hurt you to know the truth. And when I…we…" She glanced to Matt and then back to Becky. "Well, I didn't mean for that to happen. But it did and I didn't know how to tell you. And when I found out I was pregnant, I knew it would destroy you."

"It wouldn't have—"

"Yes it would have." Her voice was firm but gentle. "You loved him so much and you thought you had it all figured out. You were going to have a life together and have babies." Nikki didn't miss Becky's flinch when she spoke. "If I announced I was pregnant, all of that would have changed. All of it." She let her words sink in for a moment before she added, "I couldn't do that to you. I loved you too much. So I left. And no, it was definitely not the coward's way out."

Becky shook her head as if she didn't want to hear what Nikki was saying. "But you could have—"

"No. I wanted you to have everything you wanted. Everything you deserved out of life. And that wouldn't have happened if I'd stayed. You didn't deserve to suffer because of my choice."

"A mistake." Matt turned to his wife, holding her by the shoulders. "I told you it was a mistake and I'd take it back if I could. Becky, I never thought in a million years this would happen. I never would have…"

Nikki stopped listening. She couldn't bear to hear his words. Yes, she'd regretted the way things happened. But she'd never once considered what she'd done with Matt a mistake. He'd been split up from Becky and the two of them had always been close. That night when he came over to talk, it wasn't like they'd been drinking or not known what they were doing. They did. They both did. Even if it wasn't the same as what he felt for Becky, Nikki knew Matt loved her. At least a little. And never would she think that what they'd done together was a mistake. Not when that one night had given her Ryan.

"I'm sorry things turned out the way they did," Nikki interrupted their private moment. "I never meant for things to play out this way."

Matt faced Nikki again, but didn't let go of Becky's hand. "We can't change the past," he said. "But we can change how we go forward from here. We'd really like to meet Ryan."

"Before you leave," Becky added.

"Leave?"

Nikki looked at the ground and kicked at a chunk of ice. "I have to go home," she said.

"You can't leave," Matt said. "Not now."

"I have a job," she said. "A life. Ryan has school." Even as she spoke the words, she knew it was a lie. Sure, she had a job and Ryan had school. But they could do those things anywhere. She wouldn't admit it, not even to herself, but she didn't have anything real to go back to. Not really.

"When are you leaving?"

"Right after Mom's service," Nikki said. "We really have to get back."

"Before the festival?" Becky sounded horrified. "No. You have to stay. It's tradition."

"I haven't been in years, Becky." Nikki wrapped her arms around herself, the chill starting to get to her. "It's hardly my tradition."

"Then we'll start a new one."

Nikki tried to smile at her friend's eagerness, and her open heart, so willing to accept them. A motion from the corner of her eye caught her attention. The ice carving was taking place on the far side of the square and she knew Levi and Ryan were there watching. It was too soon. She couldn't risk them running into Becky and Matt. Not yet. A knot in her stomach formed at the thought of telling Ryan about his dad. Obviously, it wasn't something she could put off much longer. "Look," she said, the need to be away from them overwhelming her. "I can't deal with this right now." Unwanted tears sprang to her eyes and she blinked hard, hoping they wouldn't notice. "Everything that's been going on, I just can't...look, I need to talk to Ryan first."

"We can—"

"No." She held up her hand, cutting Matt off. "I need to talk to him first. He's only a kid and this is a lot to take in." She swiped at her face and sniffed loudly. "I'll tell him," she added, more to convince herself than Becky and Matt. "Just promise me you'll leave him alone until I do."

"Nikki," Becky started. She took a step forward as if she was going to, what? Hug her? Fortunately, she stopped before the moment got any more awkward. "We'll figure this out," she said. "Together."

Nikki's first instinct was to snap back at her. She wanted to tell Becky that it wasn't her problem to figure out. But that would be a lie. The secret was out. She had an overwhelming fear over how Ryan would react to the truth, but as she nodded, turned and walked away, there was also a sense of relief that washed over her. Secrets were a heavy load to carry and with her mom gone, there was no one left to help.

###

AFTER LEAVING Matt and Becky standing in the square, Nikki didn't know what to do with herself. Ryan would still be a few hours with Levi and even though the loneliness was overwhelming her, she wouldn't ruin his day. He'd been so excited when Levi offered to take him to watch the ice carvers. He was just a boy and he needed a little fun. Lord knows she wasn't very much fun to be around lately. Not with everything. Besides, for everything Halfway wasn't, it was a very fun little town that knew how to throw a festival. Ryan would have a good day.

Nikki found herself walking aimlessly down the main street, staring in the windows of the shops she used to know so well. There were a few changes, but there was enough that was familiar that Nikki instantly felt comfortable. No matter how long she'd been gone, Halfway was home. Nowhere else she'd lived since leaving had ever had the same feeling. Even the small townhouse they lived in now, with the neatly groomed yard and bike lying in the walk, didn't feel as right as Halfway did.

She'd told Becky and Matt she had to get back. But the truth was, she worked from home. Designing websites was a pretty portable job and it had been perfect for a single mom with no one to depend on. She'd been able to create a successful little business on her own while being available for Ryan. Of course, a home office had its own set of drawbacks. She didn't get out very much. Not unless you counted a PTA meeting. And Nikki didn't. She couldn't remember the last time she'd had a date, either. And she knew that wasn't fair. Ryan deserved a father in his life.

A pang of guilt hit her as she remembered the look on Matt's face.

Ryan had a father.

She pushed those thoughts out of the way. She'd tell Ryan later. She said she would do it, and she would. She'd made enough mistakes, and she didn't need to compound them. But she also wasn't going to let Becky and Matt pressure her into doing it before either of them was ready. No. She knew her son better than anyone else in the world. She'd do what was best.

"Hey, careful."

At the last minute, Nikki sidestepped a man carrying a large box with pine boughs sticking out the top.

"I'm so sorry," the man behind the box said. "I can't see very well around this thing." He shifted his load and looked at her. "Nikki Landon?"

She smiled at the familiar voice. "Oh my God, Parker? Is that you?"

Parker Rhodes put the box down on the sidewalk and in the next instant, pulled Nikki into a crushing hug. His arms were warm, and strangely enough, he smelled the same way he had in high school, like fresh cut flowers. Despite herself, Nikki closed her eyes and enjoyed the moment of familiarity and comfort.

When he released her, Parker took a step back and said, "I heard you were in town and I'm so sorry about your mother. Levi has the shop doing all the arrangements for the service, and…I'm sorry."

"Don't be. I'm glad you're doing the flowers." Parker's family had always run the local flower shop, which meant on the few dates they'd had, he'd always presented her with the most beautiful flower arrangements. "And obviously, you're still at the shop. How are your parents?"

"Dad passed a few years back, but Mom's still doing the

arranging. I help out where I can, but I'm teaching at the high school now. Can you believe it? In the very halls where we used to get in trouble. I'm the one handing out the detentions now. It's pretty crazy."

Nikki laughed and surprised herself by feeling lighthearted for the first time in days. Parker's presence always did have that effect on her, but she'd been too consumed with her feelings for Matt to notice when they were kids. "It's so good to see you," she said genuinely.

"I can't think of anyone I would've preferred to run into myself." Parker smiled and his green eyes crinkled up at the edges the way they used to. "Hey. Do you have time for a coffee? Or maybe a hot chocolate? I just need to run these boughs over to the square, but then I'd love to catch up."

"Oh, I..." She shifted from foot to foot. "Are you sure you don't have to be home for dinner or anything?"

He laughed. "I'm sure my dog can eat without me. He's pretty self-sufficient that way."

"You're not married?" She'd just assumed that a great guy like Parker would have been snatched up by now. Especially in a small town like Halfway. Just because she'd been too preoccupied to notice how amazing he was back in high school didn't mean every other girl hadn't wanted to be with him.

Parker shook his head. "I never did get over you, Nikki. You ruined me for any other."

Nikki joined in his laughter, enjoying the lighthearted flirting. "Uh huh, you smooth talker, you."

"So yes to the coffee?"

She glanced at her watch. Levi said he'd get Ryan a hotdog from the cafe for dinner, so she had at least another hour before she needed to be home. Besides, it would be nice to spend some time thinking about anything else but her real life, and she couldn't deny the draw she felt towards Parker.

She nodded and grinned. "Absolutely."

CHAPTER 12

~Becky~

THE AIR WAS brisk as they walked hand in hand to the cafe for their long-delayed hot chocolate. It took four hours to get it all right, but at least when she called her mother tonight, she could say that all the lights worked.

The cafe was crowded by the time they'd completed all the little things that needed to be taken care of in the park but Becky managed to snag a table in the far back corner while Matt ordered two hot chocolates at the counter. She wasn't sure why they came in and sat when they probably should have headed home to have their talk, but Matt insisted.

"Here you go, peppermint mocha and a biscotti." Matt handed her the mug before he sat down. The silence lengthened between them as they sat there sipping their drinks. Becky smiled at various people who came into the cafe for their own hot beverage but quickly glanced away if they seemed inclined to come and talk to them.

"Do you think he was there?" Matt finally broke the silence between them.

She shrugged. "I would imagine so, but I doubt I'd recognize him even if he stood right next to me."

"You would. He's the spitting image of how I looked at his age." A soft smile grew across his face and the anxiety that had lingered in his eyes disappeared. "I wish my parents had known about him." The wistfulness to his tone, the longing stuck a dagger in Becky's heart.

She reached across the table and placed her hand over his. "I'm sorry, Matt. I'm sorry that we never had a baby for them to hold, to see smile or even to spoil as he or she got older." She rubbed his hand while he stared at the table. He blinked a few times before he looked at her.

"And I'm sorry that you missed out on all of that with Ryan," she said.

"I'm a father," Matt whispered. He turned his gaze upwards and Becky caught sight of the tears that pooled in his eyes.

That's what she loved most about Matt. His soft heart. He cried during commercials and his heart broke along with anyone else's if they experienced a loss. He was kind, gentle, and yet a giant at the same time.

"Yes, yes you are." She could put her hurt aside for the moment. Maybe it was time to stop looking inward and feeling sorry for herself for not being able to give Matt something he'd always desired—something he already had.

"How could I not know? Aren't you supposed to know these things as a parent?"

Becky didn't respond. She didn't really need to. She had no idea what you were supposed to know or not know as a parent. This was new territory for her, for them.

"You know now." She took a sip of her mocha. "How did you find out?"

Matt glanced behind him, out onto the street. "It was when I dropped those boxes off. I saw him and knew right away."

Becky tried to smile, but she couldn't. She suddenly had an image of Matt with Nikki and it sent shivers down her spine. That also explained why he'd come home unnerved that day and she couldn't figure out what had been wrong. She struggled not to show her emotions in her face. Even then, when he'd first found out, he'd kept it a secret from her. She swallowed past the hurt.

"Honey, I'm so sorry. It's the one thing I've regretted the most since the moment it happened." He must have caught the tremble of her hands.

"You should have told me." There was nothing else she could say. Her mom was right. They were broken up when it happened and it was in the past. Now is what mattered. Them. Their marriage. The fact they now have a son they never knew about.

"I should have. I can't…I don't even…" Matt struggled to get the words out. She knew what he was trying to say, knew where his heart was. Making him say it out loud was just torture. So she stopped him.

"It's okay." She gave her head a slight shake. "It's in the past and as much as I think I would like to know all the details, I really don't. It's enough to know it happened. I wish it hadn't, but it did. Just do me a favor, don't belittle what happened. Earlier, you said it had been a mistake—"

"And it was," Matt interrupted her.

Yes, it had been, but he didn't see the expression on Nikki's face when he said that in front of her. She obviously didn't see it that way. She didn't doubt Nikki's words about the feelings she'd had for Matt and if truth be told, Becky hadn't been as oblivious of those feelings as she might have pretended to be. But she didn't want to acknowledge them back then either.

"But there had to have been feelings involved for you to sleep with her." She held up her hand as Matt moved to object. "No, we don't need to go there, but I just don't want you to negate something that did happen. And…no matter what, Ryan was not and will never be a mistake. Not to Nikki."

"Or to me," he said. "Not now that I know." Matt lifted her hand and brought it to his lips and placed a small kiss in her palm. "I love you."

She just smiled. "So, what do we do now?"

"We wait, I guess." He scrubbed the back of his neck. "I don't know what else we can do. She asked for time."

"What if she leaves?"

"She won't. She can't. She wouldn't skip her mother's funeral."

Becky rubbed her eyes and pinched the top of her nose. "She could. She ran once, remember? And we have no idea where she lives. She could leave with Ryan and there's nothing you could do to stop her." Part of her was worried that was exactly what Nikki would do—leave.

"Not if I have anything to do about it." Levi's friendly voice startled them both. He pulled up a chair and sat down. "That girl isn't going anywhere, not with that little boy."

"What do you mean?" Matt leaned forward and pushed his coffee mug out of the way.

"We all need to grow up one time or another. Anyone with eyes can see he's your child and running isn't the answer anymore. Not for her and not for that little boy of yours. He needs a man in his life, a father."

"He's got one." Becky squeezed her husband's hand.

"That little girl has had to think alone for long enough. Marie should have put a stop to it a long time ago. I'll never understand why she didn't."

Becky sat back as she caught the haunted look in Levi's eyes. For as long as she'd known him, he'd been a staple of the community, a solid fixture. But today, he looked…old and happy at the same time. It didn't make sense to her.

"I've loved that woman since the day I first laid eyes on her. But her daughter always came first. She should have known I would have loved Nikki as if she were my own." He cleared his throat. "I thought maybe when you girls went off to school I might have a chance, but when Nikki left so suddenly and Marie went away on those road trips of hers for lengths at a time, I knew I'd have to bide my time. I knew there was something, something she wasn't telling me...but it wasn't until I saw that little boy that I knew." He smiled at Matt. "He's something, that boy. She did a good job raising him. I know this has to be tough and no doubt there's a lot of anger inside you right now, but he's a good kid." He dipped his head down to his chest and thumped his heart.

"I don't know how I'm feeling right now, to be honest, Levi," Matt admitted, his voice low. "My life"—he glanced at Becky—"*our* lives just changed without warning. I'm angry that I lost out on ten years, I'm amazed to discover I'm a father, guilt is eating away at me for keeping what happened between Nik and me a secret..." His Adam's apple bobbed. Becky knew he was struggling to contain the tears.

"Let go of that guilt. It's not a part of this right now. We'll deal with that later. Right now, this is about Ryan." Becky knew in her heart it was the right thing to do—to focus on what was important and to let the other stuff fall by the wayside.

"You're a good man, Matthew Jennings. A good man. I'm proud to call you friend." Levi pushed his chair back and cleared his throat. "You two," Becky smiled when he leaned over and placed his hand on her shoulder, "you will make good parents to that special boy."

As Levi walked out of the cafe, Becky toyed with the word in her mind. *Parent*. Most parents have months to prepare for their child to enter their lives, but they only had days, if that. It's one thing to know about Ryan, but another to be a parent. Would she love him? Could she love him? What if she couldn't? What if she saw Nikki and the betrayal in his face every time she looked at him?

Oh God, that made her sound horrible. A monster. Ryan wasn't one of the children in her Sunday School class—he was her husband's child. Matt said he was his spitting image, so she knew she'd fall in love with him the minute she saw him. How could she not? And Nikki…she had to be a good mother. Becky knew that deep in her soul.

She would love this boy with all her heart. And, if this was the only child she ever had, then that had to be enough. It had to be.

CHAPTER 13

❄

~*Nikki*~

THE DAY WAS OVERCAST; the clouds that hung over the town were heavy with the threat of snow and absolutely perfect for a funeral. The weather matched Nikki's mood as she zipped herself into her black dress and pulled her hair back in a bun. When she was ready, she walked down the hall to see whether Ryan needed any help with his tie.

Nikki peeked into his room. "Hey, buddy, are—"

He wasn't there.

"Ryan?"

With a quick scan around the guest room, which Ryan had taken over, it was clear he wasn't hiding anywhere in the sparsely decorated space. He must already be downstairs. They only had thirty minutes or so before they needed to start making their way to Levi's. And even if she'd spent her morning procrastinating and packing for their planned departure tomorrow, Ryan had actually been mostly dressed for hours. He seemed oddly excited for the service.

But then again, to a little boy who'd never been to a funeral before, his expectations of what was actually going to happen were probably very different from reality. Nikki was just about to go down the stairs, when a noise coming from her mother's room captured her attention. She backtracked quickly and pushed the door open.

Ryan was sitting cross-legged on his grandmother's bed, staring at the wall of pictures Nikki hadn't brought herself to take down yet.

"Do you think she knows that today's her funeral?" Ryan asked without turning around.

The question caught her off guard and it took Nikki a few moments to form a response. She crossed the room and sat on the floral bedspread next to him. "I'd like to think that wherever she is, she's watching us and yes," Nikki said, "I think she knows it's her funeral today. In fact, I bet she's looking forward to the celebration she's planned. Grandma always did like a party."

"She did?" Ryan asked. "I never knew that."

Nikki's chest squeezed, seeming to compress her heart at his words. Of course he'd never known that. Ryan had never had the chance to see the way his grandma liked to organize events, and work the room, smiling and laughing with her friends. *Just like at the Tree Festival*, she thought, but before the idea could take root, she pushed it out of her head. *No.* No matter what Becky and Matt said, she wouldn't be going to the Tree Festival.

"She used to tell me I looked just like my dad."

Nikki's breath caught in her throat and she had to remind herself to breathe. She stared at her son, looking for any kind of indication that he knew the truth, any hint that he'd already figured it out. But there was nothing. He kept staring at the wall in front of him.

"I didn't know you used to talk about that with Grandma," she said when she felt more in control of herself. She knew she had to tell Ryan the truth. That's all she'd thought about as she'd packed and organized and basically thrown herself into everything that could keep her distracted from the reality of what she had to do. But no matter what logical argument she used against herself, no matter how many ways she played out the scenario in her head, she couldn't bring herself to do it. Not yet. Not before they buried his grandmother.

She stared at her son's profile. So much like his father's it made her heart hurt. Everyone else would see it in only a few hours. Nobody in Halfway would be able to ignore the resemblance. She was a fool for thinking she could walk into a room of people who'd known her and Matt their whole lives and hide anything.

"You do," Nikki said before she could change her mind. "You look just like him. Sometimes when I look at you, I think I'm seeing him when he was your age."

Ryan turned away from the wall and looked at her, his eyes shining with excitement. "Really? You knew him when you were kids?"

"I've known him my whole life, buddy." She smiled even though she wanted to cry. "And there's something I should tell you. I think you're finally old enough to know."

"My dad? You're going to tell me his name?" He bounced up onto his knees, reminding Nikki of the child he really was. She could have cried at his innocence, his blind faith that everything would not only be okay but be better than before as soon as he found out who his father was. He had no idea that his entire world would change in a few hours.

"I thought maybe I should wait until after the service." Ryan's face fell with disappointment and she added, "But, even though the timing is less than perfect, I think you should know." She paused and took a deep breath. She'd thought about this moment in her head for years. Planned out what she might say, how he'd react. How they'd move on afterwards. She'd never intended to keep the truth from him for so long. But she'd also never intended him to find out like this. Nikki exhaled. "Your dad will be there today."

She squeezed her eyes shut, not wanting to see the excitement in her son's eyes. She'd always wanted to be enough for him. And for a few years, she thought maybe she was. She counted to five in her head, waiting for his squeal of delight. His excitement.

Nothing.

Nikki opened her eyes to see Ryan staring at her blankly. "Ryan?" She reached out to touch his arm, to feel a connection with him. "Are you okay?"

After a moment, he nodded. "He's here? In this town?"

"Yes. He lives here."

"And I can meet him? For real?"

"Yes." Nikki swallowed hard. "For real."

Ryan nodded again, his face a mask of seriousness. "Okay."

"Are you going to be okay, buddy? I mean, if you don't want to—"

"I do." He grabbed her arm and she had to swallow a genuine smile at the enthusiasm he was trying to hide. "I mean, if it's okay."

"Of course it's okay." Nikki pulled her son into her arms and held him tightly. She stroked his silky blond hair and tried to hold the tears back as she repeated, "Everything will be okay. It'll all be okay." But she couldn't be sure who she was trying to convince: Ryan or herself.

###

HALF THE TOWN must have turned out for her mom's service and as Nikki peeked out of the back room that was reserved for families only, she tried to slow her breath and not hyperventilate at the idea of walking through that room full of people from her past. People who knew her and had known her for her whole life.

She turned and looked at Ryan, who was studying the program Levi had printed out. His little shoulders were hunched over and every few moments, she could see his body shake a bit, as if he was holding in his tears. Nikki's heart broke for her son. There'd been too much sadness and confusion in his young life. Way more than there should have been.

She sat down next to him and slid her arm around his small shoulders. "I know it's tough, buddy. It's never easy to say goodbye." He looked up into her eyes and Nikki had to pull on strength she didn't know she had to keep from crying at the pain she saw there. "But we have to remember that it's not really about saying goodbye today. It's more of a celebration of her life and what a great woman she was. You should see all the people out there. A lot of people loved Grandma. I wish you could have known her here."

"In Halfway?"

She nodded. "She was really something." She smiled, remembering the way everyone in town would stop and want to chat no matter where they were. Her mother had a way about her that made people want to open up and spill their problems. When she was younger, it would irritate Nikki to no end that they'd always be late wherever they were going, or she'd have to pretend not to be listening while she waited for her mom to finish giving advice or offering a shoulder to cry on, or even just a hug. "Everyone liked her," Nikki said, swallowing the lump in throat.

"Why didn't we ever come visit?" Ryan shifted until he was facing her. "When she was alive, I mean. We never came."

It wasn't the first time she'd heard the question, and it definitely wasn't the first time she'd given the same answer. She opened her mouth to repeat it, but no words came out. Fortunately, before Ryan could push the issue, Levi walked into the room.

He placed his big hand on Nikki's shoulder and said, "Are you ready? It's time to start."

Nikki nodded. "Are you ready to do this, buddy?"

Like the little man he was becoming, Ryan jumped to his feet and straightened his jacket. "I'm ready, Mom."

"Hey." Levi put his hand on Ryan's shoulder. "Why don't you run to the bathroom so I can talk to your mom for a minute?"

Ryan glanced between them and then did as he was told. When the door closed behind him, Levi turned to Nikki. "How you doing, kiddo? Are you ready for this?"

"Can you ever be ready to say goodbye to your mom?"

He put his hand on her shoulder and squeezed. "I wasn't talking about your mom."

Nikki looked at her feet and twisted her hands. She knew exactly what he was talking about. "That's going to be hard, too. Really hard."

"You're doing the right thing and everyone is going to understand."

"No." Nikki shook her head. "No one is going to understand." She swung around, determination in her eyes. "But I don't care. I'm sick of running. I'm sick of hiding my son. It's not fair to him, it wasn't fair to my mom, and—"

"It's not fair to you, Nikki."

"That doesn't matter."

"Yes," Levi said, his voice soft. "It does. And I hope this means that you're staying. Going to give that boy a home."

"He has a home. He's always had a home."

"This is his home, Nikki. He belongs here. You both do."

Her head spun with what he was saying and what was waiting for them beyond the walls of the private room. It was easy for Levi to think that everything would be okay and the citizens of

Halfway would accept them with open arms. But he wasn't the one who had to face them.

Just then, Ryan came out of the bathroom and Nikki knew she couldn't put it off any longer. She held her hand out for her son, took a deep breath and nodded her head at Levi. "Let's do this."

Whatever was going to happen, and no matter how people were going to react, Nikki didn't care. She couldn't. Today was about her mom and her son. And that was all that mattered.

The moment they walked in, the room fell silent and all eyes were on Nikki and Ryan as they made their way down the aisle to the front row. She tried to ignore the gentle murmuring that started up and wrapped her arm around Ryan a little tighter, wanting to shield him from the whispering and rumors that would undoubtedly start to spread through the crowd. When they got to the front of the room, she made Ryan sit first, so she could sit on the end and block him from view. When she was settled, she glanced over to her left and directly into the eyes of Matt, who was watching them intently. Averting her gaze, she caught the way Becky's pretty face was clouded with hurt, and she saw the tears swimming in her eyes.

She knew that although Becky was probably sad for the real reason they were there, that wasn't the reason for the tears. She couldn't move her gaze from Ryan, and Nikki couldn't even begin to imagine what was going through her friend's head. She averted her eyes and focused on Levi, who was starting the service.

Somehow she made it through the next forty-five minutes. Her mother and Levi had done a beautiful job of designing the service and choosing the songs. But not even her mother could have planned the amazing speeches and tributes her friends and neighbors prepared for her. They brought tears to her eyes, but she wouldn't let them spill. She had to stay strong for Ryan because the hardest part of the day hadn't even started yet.

As soon as the final hymn began to play, Levi closed his book, left it on the table and walked down the aisle, stopping in front of her. She blinked and took his outstretched hand, gratefully gripping it like an anchor in the swirling sea of chaos. She tucked her arm in his and took Ryan's hand, letting Levi lead them through the room. She could feel everyone's eyes on them as they made their way slowly. The urge to flee was strong. But she could feel Becky and Matt's eyes watching her. She glanced down at her son, tears streaking his face, and she knew she couldn't run. As much as she wanted to leave all the heartache behind her, she owed it to her little boy.

She took a deep breath, fortifying herself and moved into the reception area where everyone would gather to offer her condolences, eat finger sandwiches, and sip tea. She could handle the well-wishers; she just hoped she could handle Matt and Becky.

CHAPTER 14

~*Becky*~

HE REALLY WAS *Matt's son.* That's the only thing Becky could think when she first caught sight of Ryan as he walked down the aisle with Nikki. Her chest hurt as she struggled to contain all the emotions that threatened to break loose. She reached for Matt's hand and held tightly as she struggled to not stare. From the little curl in his hair to the shade of blue in his eyes, there was no doubt. And from the low murmur behind her, she knew others had noticed too.

Matt's legs twitched beside hers, and she knew he wanted to go over and sit with his son, introduce himself and just be there. She also knew that he heard the voices behind them as well.

She forced herself to focus on Levi, who stood at the front, but it was difficult. She glanced over at her mother, who sat in her wheelchair at the end of the pew and tried to smile at her. She'd had a long talk with Norma earlier today as she signed her out of the hospital and took her home.

"Today is a time to celebrate Marie's life. To honor her love for her family, for her friends, and for this town. She was the mother everyone wanted, the friend you never thought you deserved, the woman with a heart large enough to take every stray in and love them as her own." Levi had put down his paper and spoke from his heart.

Becky struggled to listen to his words, knowing how difficult today must be for him. But it was hard. All she could think about was afterwards. Surely afterwards Nikki would let Matt spend some time with his son, introduce them and not hide Ryan away anymore. She had to. Right?

Norma had warned her not to rush things, especially today. They were here to honor Marie, not to guilt Nikki into staying in town so Matt could be with his son, no matter how much Becky had wanted that to be the case. A million arguments rolled through her mind, things she could say to Nikki to help her see reason, but they all ended up being lame and selfish.

Look at it through Nikki's heart, her mother had advised. And she'd tried. She really, really had, but she couldn't. She would never have left, not like that, not without saying goodbye first. Nor did she think she had the strength to raise a child, all alone, without ever once asking for help. As much as she hated to admit it, Becky was a homebody at heart. She would have stayed, faced the criticism of being a pregnant and unwed teenager and figured out a way to make it work.

Nikki's reasons for leaving the way she had hurt more ways than she'd wanted to admit. What kind of a friend had she been to Nikki back then? Had she really been that shallow? That selfish?

As she listened to the stories that people told of Marie, how one woman had touched their lives in a way that would never be forgotten, Becky knew that if today had been her funeral, those same stories wouldn't have been said.

When Uncle Dennis stood and shuffled his way out past her

mother's wheelchair, Becky wondered what story her uncle would have to share, so she was caught a little off guard when he began to push Norma towards the front.

Tears smarted in her eyes as she watched her mother unfold a sheet of paper and place it in her lap.

"If Marie were here today, she'd be telling us all to shush up and enjoy a piece of her homemade baking. If there ever was a woman who hated to be praised, it was her. And yet, I don't think I've ever known a woman who deserved it more."

Becky caught the way Levi smiled as he sat beside the podium.

"Marie saved my life, literally, and in more ways that I could even describe. She was there for me when I lost my babies all those years ago. She stood by me as I watched Levi here lower my husband's body into his grave and she sheltered me as best she could before we were hit by that truck on the road. Those last few moments together," her mother's voice caught, "they play through my mind, over and over. We were talking about our daughters, and how proud of them we were." Norma smiled at Becky before she turned her attention to Nikki. "Girl, your mother loved you with all her heart. You were her reason for getting up every day and doing everything she did, even though you were living somewhere else. There wasn't a mother more proud of her daughter than Marie."

As Norma paused, the sound of sniffles filled the room. Becky reached for a new tissue from the box beside her as she watched her mother compose herself.

"I lost my sister that day. I wish there had been something I could have done to stop her death. Maybe I could have stopped for that coffee she'd suggested instead of wanting to rush home after our shopping trip, or even traded places with her even though I knew she was too tired to drive. She saw that truck first, but rather than try to protect herself, she leaned over and sheltered my body with hers even as the truck hit us." Norma's head dropped and her hands twisted together in her lap as she sat there, in front of everyone, struggling not to cry.

"Tomorrow is our town's Tree Festival and you all know how much Marie loved our annual tradition. Even though she won't be there with us in person, her spirit will be and I know she would be so proud of the fact that our two daughters had worked on it together." She smiled at Becky and then raised her chin. "I'm not saying goodbye today. I don't believe in them. I'll be seeing my best friend soon enough. She knows how I like things to be done, so I'm sure after she's done her exploring of heaven up there, she'll be working on getting things ready for me. But until that day, I don't plan to waste one more moment—if anything is to be taken from this day, from the stories told by everyone here, it's that we all need to be more like Marie, and that's exactly what I plan to do. Starting now."

Becky leaned her head against Matt's shoulder at her mother's words. She was right, as usual. She looked up at her husband and mouthed *I love you* to him as Levi ended the service with one of Marie's quotes and then the final instructions Marie had given him.

"Now, you all know Marie loved a good party, so please, if you'll all join us in the reception hall, there are platters of Marie's favorite sandwiches and treats, as well as a special gift for everyone. There's a table as you enter with these gifts. Please, take one. But don't open it. What Marie would like is for you to give that little gift to someone else—someone not here today. The idea is to spread a little bit of love around, and what better time than this, during the holiday season."

Levi headed down the aisle, but stopped beside Nikki and offered her his arm. Becky's heart broke for her old friend. Nikki's face had blanched and there was a hollow look to her eyes as she reached towards Levi. She held her other hand out and waited for her son to take it and then walked beside Levi towards the back of the room. Becky waited for Matt to stand, but he didn't move; he just sat there, his body angled to watch Nikki and Ryan. There was an uncomfortable silence in the room before Matt turned around and focused on the front. Becky looked behind her and nodded to the people who watched them with concerned glances.

"Matt, we should go," Becky whispered. As if in a daze, Matt stood. She couldn't read what was going through his mind, but she could imagine. She reached for his hand and pulled him down towards the other end of the pew where her mother waited.

With bags beneath her eyes, Norma looked as if she was ready to fall asleep. "Do you want Uncle Dennis to take you home?" Just fresh out of the hospital, her mother did not need to be overdoing it, no matter how much medication she was on.

"Not yet. But when I'm ready, Dennis will take me home, don't worry."

"I do worry. You need to be resting."

"I'll rest when I'm dead." Norma's lips thinned. "Just remember what I said earlier. Don't force things in there. Let Nikki make the first move."

Becky glanced at Matt. He wasn't paying them any attention. "I'm not sure if that's even possible. I don't think Matt will see anyone else in the room but his—"

"Then make it possible," Norma interrupted. "This is not the time. There's enough pressure on her as it is. Don't you think others are going to be seeing the connection?"

Becky's shoulders dropped. Everyone knew, the moment Nikki had walked down the aisle with her son, that he was Matt's. They'd have to be blind not to see the resemblance.

"Come on." Matt pulled her arm. "It's time." Becky doubted he'd heard a single word her mother had said. She followed him out of the room and into the reception area, where everyone stood, waiting for this moment.

. . .

###

THE LOOK NIKKI gave Becky as she stood at the other end of the reception hall surrounded by people who only wanted to wish her well reminded Becky of a time from when they'd been kids attending a summer camp.

Nikki's name had been called to take part of an impromptu skit during their nightly fire camp time. Not one to bask in the spotlight, Nikki had frozen while everyone started to chant her name.

She looked the exact same way right now. Frozen. A weak smile was plastered on her face and she had her arm wrapped around her son's shoulders. Becky could tell she wanted to get away from those who surrounded them but couldn't.

So Becky reacted as only she could. She dropped Matt's hand and marched across the room to her friend's defense, calling out her name in a loud voice.

"Nikki." She had no idea what she was going to say but anything would work. "My…"—she glanced around the room and saw Norma by the door—"mom is going to be heading home soon. I don't think you've seen her yet since you've been home." She nudged her way between a couple who were giving pointed stares at Ryan and hooked her arm through her friend's. "Excuse us," she said as they shouldered past.

"Thank you," Nikki whispered.

"Don't mention it. And don't mention how tired my mom looks either when you see her. She was just released this morning but you know her…" Her voice drifted off as they stopped in front of Norma.

Nikki dropped down to her knees and reached for Norma's hand.

"I'm so sorry I haven't been by to see you," she said. "I was too…"

"Shhh, it's okay. I know." Her mother leaned forward slightly and rested her free hand against Nikki's cheek. She glanced over at Ryan and gave a soft smile. "Now, before we both get too muddled with tears, why don't you introduce me to this young man?"

Becky took a step back and gave her mother a questioning glare. *What happened to letting Nikki take the lead?*

"This is Ryan, my son." Nikki's voice grew in strength as she stared at the boy. She raised herself off her knees and placed her arm around Ryan's shoulders.

"Well now." Norma sat back and placed her hands together in her lap. Her head tilted to the side and then she chuckled. "You remind me of your grandma, did you know that? I think it's the nose and maybe the smile, but I'm not sure about that. I'd have to see it first." Her eyes sparkled as Ryan looked up at Nikki in surprise.

"I do?" he said.

Nikki nodded. "You do. I never noticed that before."

"Now," Norma held out her plate to Ryan, "why don't you be a good boy and go get me a few more of those brownies and anything else that looks sweet. I've been eating hospital food for too long." Ryan looked at his mom for approval before he took the plate and made his way to the table.

Becky found herself turning to watch him. She told herself it was to make sure no one else bothered him while Norma was talking to Nikki but she knew it was also because she wouldn't have been able to keep her eyes off him even if she'd tried.

This is Matt's son. She still couldn't believe it.

"Did my mother ever say anything about..." Nikki's voice trailed off.

"About her grandchild? No." Norma shook her head. "She kept your secrets, child."

"I'm sorry."

"You don't need to apologize to me. I'm sure you both had

your reasons. God knows, I have my share of secrets too." Norma reached out and grabbed hold of both Nikki's and Becky's hand. Becky's stomach churned. She had no idea what her mother was doing. "Between your mother and me, we had one regret and that was the fallout between you two. It was something we'd been talking about that day as well, how we wish you two would find a way back to each other. I know there is a lot of hurt and distance between you two, but please, try to find a way to make it work. If not for yourselves, then for Marie and that little boy you've got." Norma dropped their hands, cleared her throat and swiped at the tears that flowed down her weathered cheeks as Ryan came to stand beside his mother and handed her a plate that overflowed with sweets.

"This is exactly what I needed, thank you." Norma reached out for the plate and smiled. "Now I think it's time for Dennis to take me home. I'm a bit tired."

Becky leaned down and placed a soft kiss on her mother's cheek. "Do you want me to stop in before we head home?"

"No need. Just come by in the morning to pick me up." Before Dennis wheeled her away, she placed her hand on Ryan's arm. "You come see me tomorrow, by the big tree, okay? I have something for you that was your grandmother's."

"But we..." Nikki's voice trailed off as Dennis pushed Norma out of the reception room.

"Don't say you won't be there." Becky turned to face her friend. "You have to be there. Ryan would love it." She smiled down at Matt's son.

At Nikki's sharp intake of breath, Becky turned just as Matt came to stand at her side.

"Would like what?" he said.

Trying to act nonchalant, Becky gave Matt a bright but tense smile. "I was saying how much Nikki's son would love the festival tomorrow." She hoped he understood the undercurrent going on between them. Becky would do anything and everything she could to get Nikki to stay, even if just for an extra day.

Matt's eyes narrowed. "You're not thinking of leaving, are you?"

Before Nikki could respond, Ryan stepped in front of his mom and faced her. "But we can't. Grandma's friend said she had something for me."

"And there's a lot of kids' activities planned that Ryan should enjoy," Becky interjected while Nikki shook her head.

"I don't...there's still so much..." Nikki sighed in defeat. "We'll see, okay?" She gave a pointed look to both Becky and Matt while she ruffled Ryan's hair. He stepped back from her touch and attempted to fix his hair without looking embarrassed and Becky struggled not to smile. A boy trying to be a man.

There was an awkward silence between the four of them before Ryan took a good look at Matt and smiled.

"You came over to the house, didn't you? You're mom's friend."

Matt smiled. "Sure am. I've known your mom since she was... well, I've known her my whole life."

"Your whole life?" When Ryan looked at Nikki, Becky almost choked back a chuckle. You could tell mother and son had a silent language and that Ryan was practically yelling at her. Nikki winced before she glanced up at the ceiling.

"I need your help, Mom." Becky heard Nikki's soft prayer before she squatted down so she was eye level with her son and reached for his hands.

"Okay, buddy, remember how I was telling you that...well, that your...This is Matt. Your—"

"Father," both Matt and Ryan said together.

Becky choked up and had to turn her head in hopes no one would have noticed. The way they said it at the same time, combined with the look of desperation in Nikki's eyes, just about floored her. Becky felt like a bystander, someone with vivid interest in the scene before her but with little or no impact to what was happening. The look of understanding and hope that flared in Ryan's eyes broke her heart. How long had this boy wondered about his father? How long did Nikki think she could continue with the facade?

Matt held out his hand to Ryan and waited for the young boy to take it. Once he did, Matt shook it, holding tightly to his son's fingers.

"I'm Matt and this," Matt reached for Becky's hand and held tightly, "is my wife and your mother's best friend, Becky. And Ryan," Matt had to clear his voice before he could speak again, "it's really nice to finally meet you."

CHAPTER 15

❄

~Nikki~

Nikki wasn't sure how she'd feel when the truth was finally all out there. But when Matt and Ryan looked at each other, father and son finally understanding their connection with each other, Nikki did not expect the rush of emotion that crashed over her. When her knees buckled, thankfully someone was there at her side, holding her up before she could cause a scene. She turned to see who her savior had been because everyone else was intent on watching the reaction between Matt and Ryan.

"Oh," Nikki said when she saw Parker Rhodes at her side, his arm hooked under her elbow, subtly keeping her from falling. "Thank you. I didn't even know you were here." The truth was, Nikki hadn't seen anyone. She'd been so focused on saying goodbye to her mom and the impending meeting, she had barely registered the speeches, let alone the mourners in attendance.

He smiled gently. "I wouldn't miss it. Are you okay?"

Nikki nodded. "I am, thank you. It's been a rough day and,"

she gestured with her head to the little meeting that was going on next to them, "it's far from over."

"I can see that." He raised his eyebrows and Nikki knew he wouldn't press for details. He didn't have to. Certainly he could see the truth just as well as everyone else in the room. "I think you could use a tea," he said. "If you're sure you can stand on your own, I'll go grab you one."

"Thank you, Parker."

He nodded again and disappeared into the crowd, giving Nikki a chance to focus on Ryan and Matt, who had fallen into easy conversation. She should have been surprised that her ten-year-old son who'd just met his father for the first time was capable of having a casual conversation about video games, but she wasn't. That's just the way Ryan was. Just like his dad.

She let out a breath she hadn't realized she'd been holding and looked past the big smile on Matt's face to Becky. She was watching the two of them intently with a strange look on her face. But it wasn't a bad expression. Instead, Becky looked almost happy. Could she be pleased about Matt's illegitimate child? No. Not *pleased* about that, but knowing Becky, she was just happy for her husband, because there was no denying the pleasure in his face while he was talking to his child.

Thank you. Becky mouthed the words to Nikki.

Becky didn't have to thank her. *No.* Nikki shook her head. It should be her thanking Becky for being so understanding. Why was she? The Becky Nikki had known in high school would have lost her mind to find out about Ryan. This was one scene that would not have played out ten years ago.

But it wasn't ten years ago. And things changed. But could things change that much?

Nikki looked around the room at the gathering of townspeople who'd come to pay their respects. More than a few of them had noticed the scene playing out between Matt and Ryan. And no doubt they'd all put together the pieces of the puzzle. So far, no one had come to offer Nikki her condolences. They were waiting. Likely because there was more interesting things happening.

She hated that she was so cynical, but small towns were all the same and even if some things changed, they wouldn't have changed that much. She felt as if she were moving in a fog, but she turned her attention back to what Ryan and Matt were talking about. They were still on the subject of video games, and Ryan was giving Matt the detailed play-by-play of his favorite game, Minecraft.

"Have you heard of it?" Ryan asked Matt, who'd pulled up two chairs so they were sitting across from each other. "It's all about creating worlds, but there are griefers and they like to destroy everything you create. It sucks."

"I bet it does," Matt said, his voice laced with sincerity. "When I was your age, I liked to play Mario Brothers. And Bowser was always trying to destroy everything."

"Mario Brothers? No way? My friend has that one. It's so cool."

Matt laughed. "I think the game you're thinking of is a bit newer than the one I used to play."

"Would you like to play with me sometime, Da—Ma—"

Nikki froze, and she wasn't the only one. Matt's grin faded, and a look of panic came over his face, as Ryan tried to finish his sentence.

"Um," he mumbled and looked around at the adults. "What should I call you?"

Matt looked to Nikki for help, but she couldn't offer any assistance. She was still frozen to the spot. A roaring filled her head as the noise of the room seemed to pick up volume. Her legs threatened to give out again, causing her to grip the table.

Thankfully, it was Becky who saved them all from the increasingly awkward moment. "Why don't you call him Matt for now?" she suggested gently. "And you can call me Becky. This is all pretty new to all of us, so we can figure it out as we go, don't you think?"

Ryan seemed satisfied with that answer and in true ten-year-old-boy fashion, completely changed the subject. "There's cake over there. Did you know my grandma loved cake? It didn't even matter what kind it was. She liked all of it."

Nikki's eyes filled up with tears at the reminder of why they were all gathered there. "Why don't you go get some?" she suggested.

"Really?"

"Of course." She tousled his hair. "And you know what? I think I could really use some cake, too."

"But you never eat cake!"

"Well, today is an exception, I guess." She forced a smile. "And I think I'd like the biggest piece you can find me. Do you think you can do that?"

Ryan set off on his mission and suddenly Nikki didn't know what she was doing standing there with Matt and Becky. She glanced around uncomfortably, wishing someone, anyone at all, would come up to offer her a kind word about her mother, or a hug, or…

"He's amazing," Matt said.

Nikki blinked and focused on him. Matt had stood from his chair and was standing next to Becky, his arm around her waist.

"He really is, Nikki," Becky chimed in. "He's so well-spoken and such a polite little boy. I can't believe he's ten."

Silence fell over them as they all thought about her words. Of course he was ten. That was the entire reason they were all in the position they were in.

Nikki broke the tension. "Well, I'm glad you like him," she said. "He really is a good kid and so smart."

"Just like his dad was at that age," Becky said.

"Becky, I don't think…" Matt glanced at Nikki. "Is this weird?"

She nodded and answered truthfully. "Yes. But she's right.

He's so much like you. Every day I feel like I'm looking at a mini version of you. The way he talks, his interests, even the way he wrinkles up his nose when he laughs. Sometimes I wonder if there's any of me in him at all."

Nikki didn't miss the way Becky straightened and squared her shoulders. No doubt this was difficult on her. How could it not be?

"I know today is hard," Matt said. "But even with everything going on, thank you for doing this."

She shrugged. "It was time. And it's not like he didn't already figure it out, right? I told you, he's a smart kid." She looked around and saw a woman she recognized as one of her mom's many friends heading in her direction. "I really should go talk to some people. Can we continue this later?"

"Of course," Matt said and Becky nodded. They were so in tune with each other that Nikki couldn't help but feel a small pinch of envy at their closeness.

"Good." She moved to turn away when Becky's words stopped her.

"Now that we've found him," she said, "we're really looking forward to having Ryan be part of our lives. I guess we'll have to talk about what that looks like."

Icy fear pricked along her spine and a knot twisted in Nikki's stomach. Finally, unsure of how she made her head move, she nodded. "Yes," was all she said before turning away, desperate to find her son and make the rounds so she could leave and the day could be over.

###

. . .

Nikki led the way up the porch, kicking herself for not leaving a porch light on, while Parker carried a sleeping Ryan in his arms. She unlocked the door and held it as he went inside.

"You can put him down on the couch," she said. "He's probably getting heavy."

Parker shook his head and used it to gesture to the stairs.

"No," Nikki whispered. "He's too heavy—you'll hurt yourself."

With a grin, Parker hefted the sleeping boy a bit higher in his arms and headed towards the stairs. Nikki shook her head and followed after them. "First door on the right."

Parker slipped Ryan onto the bed without disturbing him. Nikki was able to pull his shoes and jacket off before covering him with his blanket. He might as well sleep in his clothes. He'd had a big day, and there was no way Nikki would risk waking him up just for pajamas.

"Come on," she whispered to Parker and ushered him out of the room, clicking the door shut behind them.

Once they were downstairs, Parker didn't make any move to leave, and suddenly the idea of being alone didn't seem all that appealing to Nikki, either. "Would you like a coffee or maybe something stronger? It's been that kind of day."

Parker laughed. "Something stronger sounds great."

In the kitchen, Nikki found a surprisingly well-stocked liquor cabinet, if you liked liqueurs, that was. She shrugged apologetically to Parker. "Sorry, it seems I only have Grand Marnier, Amaretto, and some creamy pink stuff."

"Hmm, as enticing as the creamy pink stuff sounds, a glass of Amaretto over ice would be perfect."

She poured them two glasses and they went back to the living room, where Nikki curled up on one end of the couch, pulling an afghan over her legs.

"Thank you for today," she said.

He smiled and she liked that he didn't even pretend not to know what she was thanking him for. "It's what friends do," he said. "I am truly sorry that you had to go through this today. I know when I lost my dad, it was really hard."

"Thanks, Parker. That means a lot."

They each sipped their drinks and Nikki waited for him to ask the question that had to be weighing on his mind. After a few minutes of silence, Parker said, "So, that's why you left." It wasn't a question, but Nikki nodded nonetheless.

"I knew it had to be something big," he continued. "It wasn't like you to just up and take off, and I know some people thought you were running away, but—"

"There were stories?" She asked the question even though she knew that of course there'd be a variety of rumors floating around about her departure.

Parker laughed and Nikki couldn't help but notice the way his eyes sparkled when he was relaxed. "Oh, you should have heard some of the rumors, Nik. The people of Halfway could have won awards for their creative storytelling. It really was impressive. But my favorite was that you'd run away with the carnival and eventually settled in California, where you lived in a commune."

She laughed along with him and it surprised her with how good it felt. "That was your favorite?"

"Well, I did like the idea of you being happy," he said, the laughter dying on his lips. "I always wanted you to be happy, Nik."

She looked down at her lap and rolled the glass between her hands.

"I see now that I never had a chance," Parker said softly. "It was Matt all along, wasn't it?"

Nikki nodded. "It was."

"I get it."

She looked up. "You do?"

"Well, sort of." He shrugged. "I get how you could love someone who couldn't love you back."

Nikki's heart cracked for him as she realized what he was saying. "I'm sorry, Parker. I didn't realize."

"I know you didn't." He chuckled again. "That was the whole problem. But, hey. That was a long time ago."

"It was." She nodded. It would have been so much easier if she'd fallen in love with Parker all those years ago. And then the whole mess never would have happened. But she never would have had Ryan. And despite all the drama and hurt her actions had caused, she didn't regret it. She couldn't.

"Well, I'm glad you're back." Parker raised his glass.

"Oh, I'm not back."

"You're sitting here."

"No. Well, yes. But I'm not back. Not for good."

"What about..." He tipped his head. "You can't really mean that you're going to leave. Now? What does Matt say about it?"

She shook her head. She couldn't think about it. She couldn't make a decision. Not right away. But Becky's words kept ringing in her ears. No matter how she tried to distract herself all afternoon, she couldn't stop thinking about what Becky had said. She wanted Ryan to be part of their lives, and of course she did. But how? She couldn't give up her son. The thought was terrifying. No, she wouldn't just hand Ryan over to them every second weekend. It was unthinkable.

"Hey," Parker said. He'd moved to the couch so he was sitting next to her. His hand on her arm calmed her. Nikki hadn't realized how worked up she'd gotten just thinking of the possibilities. "I didn't mean to freak you out," he said. "I just thought you would have talked about it. Or at least thought about it."

She shook her head again. "No. I didn't. I mean, I did. But not really and..." Her words were lost as sobs took over and shook her body.

Parker took her glass from her and a moment later, he pulled her into his arms. It didn't matter that they hadn't seen each other for ten years or that as sort of high school sweethearts it should have been awkward. It wasn't. And at that moment, Nikki couldn't imagine anything feeling safer than being in Parker's arms.

He stroked her hair and murmured things she couldn't make out, consoling her until her tears dried up. When she felt she might have even a basic control over herself, she pulled away and wiped at her eyes. "I'm sorry," she said. "I don't know where that came from."

"I do." He handed her a tissue from the nearby box. "You've had a hell of a day. Heck, you've had a hell of a week. Not to mention what you must have gone through as a single mom. Nikki, it's okay. You're allowed to cry."

"I know." She sniffed. "It's just that, quite honestly, I don't usually get the chance to...you know..."

"Not be strong?"

She nodded.

He handed her the glass of Amaretto again, and she took a big swallow of the cool liquid. "I know you don't want to stay," he said. "But I, for one, would really like to get the chance to spend more time with you if you do."

"How do you know I don't want to stay?"

He raised his eyebrow at her and took a sip of his drink before answering. "Besides the fact that you've said as much? It's written all over you. And did you know that I'm really good at reading people?" He grinned and his goofiness had the desired effect.

Nikki laughed. "Are you now?"

"I am," he said with mock seriousness. "Let me tell you about the time that I tried to tell Mrs. McGregor how she was feeling. She came into the shop to order some carnations, but by the time she left, I'd figured out all her secrets. And let me tell you, there are some things I don't even think Mr. McGregor knows about Mrs. McGregor."

Nikki laughed again. It felt good and she let herself get lost in Parker's stories.

###

It wasn't until she was tucked into her bed, hours later, the lingering effects of the Amaretto flowing through her veins, that she once again thought about her choices. She could follow her instinct, and take Ryan far from Halfway and from his father. He'd be upset with her; that went without saying. But he'd be with her. There would be absolutely no risk of Becky and Matt trying to take him from her. And who knew what they wanted? Could she risk it?

Nikki knew Ryan wanted to stay. At least for the festival. Especially after meeting Becky's mom and hearing she had something for him. Besides, what kid didn't like a festival? And now that he'd met his dad…but if they stayed for the festival, Ryan would for sure want to stay longer, and the longer they were here, it would only get harder to leave.

The options swirled through her head as she weighed the pros and cons of each decision. She was a mature, responsible woman. And sure, she knew what she should do. And she knew what was right. But what if what was right wasn't the right choice?

CHAPTER 16

❄

~Becky~

WITH HER HANDS wrapped tight around the mug of hot cocoa she'd just been handed by one of the volunteers, Becky made her way down through the market stalls and took the time to stop at every display and chat with those who stood behind the tables. The air was a bit nippy this morning but the weather forecast promised for bright sun and slightly warmer temperatures and Becky hoped it would be true. Even with the bright red scarf wrapped around her neck, her warm jacket and earmuffs, she was still freezing.

Unlike Matt, who wore only a long-sleeved sweater while he hefted bundled trees into place. He lifted a hand in a wave as she made her way towards him before he reached for another tree off the truck and placed it in a pile of other trees in the front of his display. If this year was like previous years, all those trees would soon be found in someone's home by the end of the night.

Becky stopped at a booth stocked with Christmas cookies and

mugs of hot water and coffee. She set her cup down and filled up a new cup with coffee for Matt. They'd barely slept last night and she knew he wouldn't say no to another dose of caffeine.

"Most of the single women are salivating right about now, watching that husband of yours."

"As long as they remain hands-off, they can look all they want." Becky smiled at Susan, who stood beside her and filled her own mug. Susan was someone she'd gone to high school with but never really gelled with. They'd nod and say hi if they passed one another in the street and were always friendly, but it would be a long time before Becky invited Susan over for dessert and coffee. "He does look good though, doesn't he?" Even after all these years, she still loved to watch him in action. Even with a sweater, his muscles were still noticeable.

"Quite a shock yesterday, seeing Nikki's son." Susan peered down at her over the rim of her coffee cup.

Becky stiffened, but forced herself to remain relaxed. They'd talked about this last night, how they would react when people brought Ryan up, because they both knew it would happen. They'd agreed that their first priority had to be protecting their family—and that included Nikki as well. They wouldn't slander her, gossip about her, or make any reference to the fact that she'd kept Matt's son away for so long.

"I'm just glad she's finally home." Becky's voice remained friendly and light before she turned and pulled out some cash. "These cookies look delicious." She reached for a plastic-wrapped tray of sugar cookies cut out in tree shapes and decorated with candy balls. "I think it's time Matt stopped for a snack and I've never known him to turn down a cookie." The girl behind the table blushed as she took the money.

"I could swear, he's the spitting image of Matt when he was a kid." Susan stuck close to her side as she left the table and made her way towards her husband.

"He's a cute kid, that's for sure," Becky agreed while inwardly groaning. Susan wasn't the type to let go of anything until she discovered every tasty morsel of gossip she could.

"So is he?"

Becky stopped. "Is he what?" She knew exactly what Susan was after. "If you have any questions, then why not ask Nikki herself? He is, after all, her child." She then left Susan behind, gaping like a dying fish with her mouth wide open as Matt waited for her at the side of the truck.

"Well, hi there, gorgeous." He leaned down and placed a kiss on her lips and then grinned while the guys on top of the truck bed started to whistle. Becky blushed like a school girl.

"Did you really have to do that?" she whispered to him.

"Kiss my wife? Sure did. Your cheeks match the color of your scarf, did you know that? So does your nose." His eyes twinkled.

Becky loved to see him like this—happy, carefree...it'd been awhile and it was all due to Ryan. He'd fairly glowed last night after they came home and it was all he could talk about. She knew he looked forward to today, to when Ryan would arrive and Matt could spend more time with him.

As she'd walked the aisles of the market, she'd kept looking for Nikki or her son and prayed they would arrive. There was a lingering fear that they might not, that Nikki would find an excuse to leave before anyone had a chance to say goodbye or discuss how their lives had changed now. She was tempted to drive over to the house and make sure Nikki would show, but when she'd mentioned it to her mother earlier, she knew it would be a bad idea.

This had to be Nikki's choice. She had to feel the freedom to make her own decision, even though essentially she was making the decision for everyone.

"Have you seen him yet?" Matt asked, his voice lowered so no one else could hear them.

Becky shook her head before she handed him the coffee and cookies. "He'll be here. It's still early."

"I know, it's just..."

"You've got trees to sell before you're allowed to go play," she teased him. "I don't want any of these trees coming home with us tonight."

"Yes ma'am." Matt dug into the cookies and took one out. He bit into it and slowly chewed it. "It's good, but not as good as yours."

"Better not be." She winked at him before she waved to the guys unloading the truck and walked away.

###

THE NEXT FEW hours passed by in a blur as Becky made her rounds through the park to see if anyone needed anything and to make sure her mother didn't overtax herself, but it warmed her heart to watch Norma smile even though she knew today would be hard. This was the first festival where Marie wasn't beside her mother, ensuring everything went smooth, and it would be the first year where their annual post-festival holiday trip to someplace warm didn't happen.

But maybe it was time to start new traditions.

She thought about the tree they'd left at home to decorate tonight. Maybe they should see whether Ryan and Nikki could come over and decorate it with them. Maybe Nikki would even help her make some cookies this year. She'd invite her mother and Uncle Dennis and make a nice evening of it.

It bothered her that she hadn't seen Nikki yet but there was still time.

"Hey beautiful." Arms wrapped around her waist as she stood at the edge of the pavilion where the local school choir was warming up to sing.

"Hey yourself. How's the tree sales?" She rested her head on his chest.

"Sold over half the trees already. But it's lunch time. Can I treat you to a sausage?"

Becky turned in his arms and laughed before they walked off, hand in hand, to where the local hotdog stand was selling farm fresh sausages. Matt had teased her this morning that he'd treat her to the best lunch in town and she should have known this was his idea of what a great lunch was, considering their freezer was stocked with these same sausages and it was Matt's favorite thing to cook on the barbecue.

As they stood in line to order, Matt suddenly dropped her arm and started to wave. She shielded her eyes to see who he was waving at and noticed Ryan standing alone.

"Go on, I'll order for us." Becky nudged him and he took off running across the park.

She caught the wide smile on Ryan's face as Matt made it to his side and then watched as they jogged back towards her. She looked around to see where Nikki was but she couldn't find her.

"Look who's joining us for lunch."

Ryan stood beside Matt with a half-smile on his face, as if he wasn't sure it was okay that he was joining them.

"I hope you like sausages, 'cause they happen to be Matt's favorite food group."

"They're not a food group." Ryan's brow rose and Becky chuckled while Matt pretended to be offended.

"Shhh. Don't say that too loudly," Becky teased. "Should I order your mom one too?"

Ryan shook his head but it was Matt who answered for him. "Nikki will be here later. She's still packing things up in the house." She knew, by the tone in his voice, that he'd really hoped she would have stuck around a little bit longer.

Once they gathered their sausages, Becky hung back while

Matt pointed out different things to Ryan in the park. This was the moment he'd been waiting for, to spend some time with his son, and although she knew she wasn't in the way, she didn't want to intrude on their time. But Matt seemed to have other ideas.

"Come on, slowpoke. Ryan has a date he doesn't want to miss." He reached for Becky's hand and pulled her along until she walked by his side. Ryan leaned forward a bit and smiled at her and she smiled back.

"That's right. My mom has something for you, doesn't she?"

Ryan's eyes widened at her words. "That's your mom?"

Becky nodded.

"So she's like, my grandmother?" he asked. A look of wonder filled his face as if he'd never thought about having an extended family now that he'd met his father.

"I guess she would be." Becky shrugged. She really wished Nikki were here right now. *How would she want this to be handled?*

"Do I call her Grandma then?"

Becky caught sight of her mother's wheelchair by the large Christmas tree in the center of the park.

"Why don't you ask her yourself?" She reached for Ryan's hand and waited till he reached out to grab hold of it.

The feel of Ryan's hand in hers caught her a bit off guard. She hadn't thought of what this would feel like, having this type of connection with him, but the moment he threaded his fingers through hers, she knew it felt right. She stared down at their joined hands and then at Matt, who smiled at her.

This was her son. Hers. No, he might not be of her blood, but he was Matt's and that was good enough. She knew the term would be stepmom, but she didn't want to think of it that way. She'd rather he be the son of her heart and right now, she had no problem imagining that to be a possible future.

Norma sat there with a box in her lap and a nostalgic look on her face as they walked towards her.

"You came," she said.

"Yes ma'am." Ryan shuffled his feet and bowed his head.

Norma's brow rose. "What's with this 'ma'am' business? You know who I am by now, don't you?"

Ryan nodded.

"Well then, let's try this again, shall we?"

Ryan blinked a few times before he looked up at Matt.

"It's okay, buddy; there's no pressure here."

It was hard for Becky to keep silent and she glanced around the park again, hoping for a glimpse of Nikki. *Where was she?* She couldn't imagine Nikki letting Ryan come here alone.

"Was my grandma really your best friend?" Ryan eyed the box in her lap.

"Did she ever tell you about me?"

Ryan nodded.

"Well, then you should know she was more than just my best friend. She was the sister of my heart. Much like your mom and my daughter were, when they were growing up."

Ryan stuck his hands in his coat pocket. "Would you mind if I called you Grandma, then, too? I…I really miss her."

A smile wreathed Norma's face as she let go of the box she held in her lap and reached both of her hands out to Ryan. He took hold of them, and she pulled him close until she gave him an awkward hug.

"This dang wheelchair. Once I'm out of it, I'll give you a proper hug, okay?" She swiped at the tears that gathered in the wrinkled folds on her cheek and smiled. "Now, I promised you that I had a gift for you. And here it is. But…" She stopped Ryan when he went to reach for it. "I want you to promise me something first."

Ryan's hands dropped to his sides. "Like what?"

Smart kid, Becky thought. She knew Matt thought the same thing when he reached for her hand and squeezed. Never promise something until you know what it is, that's what Matt always said.

Norma rolled her eyes. "Just like your father," she muttered. "All I want is for you to promise that you'll finish the thing in here that your grandmother never got to start. But," she paused, "we have to do it together. Okay?"

Becky knew right away what was in the box.

Every year, Norma and Marie would do a puzzle together. They would take turns buying a puzzle to put together but they would never open it until the day after the festival so that it would remain a surprise. Becky never understood how they could wait that long to open the gift to see what kind of puzzle it would be, but they did.

"Whose turn was it?" Becky asked.

"This," Norma cradled the box in her hands, "was Marie's gift to me. I already had mine picked out for her. I found it in the summer when you took me to that baking competition in the city." Her voice tapered off.

Becky knelt down. "Maybe you and I could do that one together?" she suggested.

"I'm confused," Ryan said.

Both Becky and Norma smiled. Norma held out the box to Ryan. "Maybe your mom can explain and then you can come see me tomorrow. A tradition is a tradition, you know. And," she looked up into the sky, "just because you are gone, doesn't mean it's okay for you to break tradition this year. Our grandson, here, will have to pick up your slack."

Ryan glanced over at Matt with a confused look on his face.

"It's okay, buddy. I think it's time Norma took some more pain meds, huh?" He gave a pointed look to Becky. "And we should probably start looking for your mom. I'm surprised she's not here yet."

Ryan's head dropped and Becky's stomach twisted. *Oh dear...*

"Ryan, where is your mom? Does she know you're here?" *Please let him say yes, please let him say yes.*

He shrugged. "Well, she knew I wanted to come here..."

Matt squatted down and looked Ryan in the eye.

"But did she know you left the house to come here?"

Silence. Becky dug out her phone and knew she needed to rectify this. She could only imagine what Nikki must be thinking right about now, wondering where Ryan was.

"Okay, so you didn't tell her you left, but she knew you had wanted to come to the festival. So she should be on her way once she realized you were gone." Matt stood. "Right?" he said as he looked at her.

"I hope so," Becky whispered. The phone rang in her ear and she tapped her leg with her free hand as she waited for the line to be picked up.

Who knows how Nikki would react. Was she still planning to leave? Would she blame her and Matt for Ryan taking off? Could this backfire on them? Would she take Ryan away from them for good?

She knew Matt was thinking the exact same thing as they both looked down at their son, who hung his head in shame.

CHAPTER 17

~*Nikki*~

Nikki dropped the last bag in the trunk of the car and headed back into the house to get Ryan. No doubt he was still angry with her for making the decision to leave instead of going to the festival. They'd had a heck of a fight and it wasn't like Ryan to yell at her or really have an outburst of any kind. He was usually such an easygoing kid. But when she'd told him her decision, he hadn't reacted well at all. After bursting into tears and arguing with her, he'd run off to his room, and instead of going after him, Nikki'd left him alone to his thoughts.

But what else could she do? After a sleepless night, she'd finally decided that she couldn't do it. As much as Ryan thought he wanted to go to the festival and see Matt and Becky, he didn't realize what that decision would really mean for them and the life they knew. She was making the right decision by leaving. At least, she hoped she was. She didn't even want to think of how Becky and Matt would react to find out she was gone. It wasn't fair to them to take off, she knew that. She wasn't totally heartless. But a mother's instincts were strong and she had to protect her baby.

Or was it herself she was trying to protect?

She paused on the porch before going inside to collect Ryan. It wasn't too late to change her mind. She could still swing by the festival on her way out of town and then...*Matt would make her stay*, she finished her own thought.

Her mind made up, Nikki pushed through the front door, hollering, "Ryan. It's time to go."

She moved through to the kitchen and surveyed everything that was left to do. She'd have to hire a company to come and pack up the rest of the house. She couldn't do it. Not if it meant staying one day longer. When she didn't hear footsteps above her, Nikki moved to the bottom of the stairs and called again.

"Ryan! Come on, buddy."

When there was still no answer, Nikki started up the stairs. With every step she took, the sense that something was wrong grew. It wasn't like Ryan to ignore her. Even if he was angry, he'd still answer her. She quickened her pace and took the stairs two at a time.

"Ryan? Come on, kiddo. Let's talk." Nikki didn't bother knocking; instead, she flung open the door to Ryan's room. "That's enough, Ryan. We need to get moving. Ryan—" The room was empty.

The hairs on the back of her neck stood up, and Nikki knew even before she searched under the bed and in the closet Ryan wasn't there. Without wasting any more time, she ran through the house, even checking the attic where Ryan had enjoyed playing the other day. But she knew he wasn't there. And with every second that passed, the feeling of dread in the pit of her stomach grew. Not because she didn't know where her son was, but because she was fairly sure she did.

Right as she was about to go flying out the door to grab him and force him to leave with her, the phone on the wall rang. She snatched it up. "Hello?"

"Nikki. Oh, thank God. I caught you." Becky's voice came over the line. "You must be going crazy."

"I am. Where's Ryan? Is he okay?"

"Of course he's okay. Why wouldn't he be?"

"I just...he's not here...and...where are you?"

"We're downtown," Becky said slowly. "Just in the main square. We'll wait here."

Nikki swirled around in the cord, twisting herself up with her mother's old-fashioned phone. She was just about to hang up when Becky added, "Oh, and Nikki?"

Nikki waited, but didn't say anything.

"He came on his own. We had nothing to do with it."

"I...I just can't—"

"But we're glad he did."

Nikki couldn't listen to any more. She hung up, grabbed her purse and was out the door a second later.

###

THE TOWN SQUARE LOOKED AMAZING. It always did for the Tree Festival. It'd been so long, Nikki'd almost managed to forget how the town of Halfway went all out for the festival that not only celebrated the season, but also their main industry. She tried not to dwell too much on the decorations, lights, and happy people everywhere she looked. Instead, she kept a keen eye out for Ryan and it wasn't long before she spotted him standing next to Matt near the town tree.

Her breath caught in her throat and she froze. *Would she ever get used to seeing them together?*

Ryan was laughing at something Matt was saying, and even

though she wasn't close enough to see it, Nikki knew that both of them would be smiling and their dimples would be on full display. Anyone with two eyes in their head could see they were father and son. And watching them together, Nikki's heart hurt. Clearly, Ryan wanted to be with Matt. He'd run away just to see him, for goodness' sake. Hot tears stung her eyes, and she hastily swiped them away. She would not cry. Not in the middle of town.

Before she could move forward, a voice startled her.

"Nikki. There you are."

Nikki spun around and looked into Becky's eyes that were full of concern and something else. Joy? That was it. She looked happy. Her whole face was glowing, and even Nikki could see it wasn't from the cool air.

"Sorry," Becky said. "I didn't mean to sneak up on you. I was just getting the boys a refill on their hot chocolate."

"The boys?" Something about the casual way Becky referred to Matt and Ryan irked her. "I hope you don't mean Ryan. Because he probably shouldn't have too much sugar. I don't like him to fill up on sweets."

Becky smiled. "Oh, surely a few cups won't hurt. It's a festival, after all."

"Yes," Nikki said. "A few cups most certainly will hurt. But I don't expect you to know that."

When she saw Becky's face fall, Nikki had a flicker of regret. She knew she was being a bitch. Becky didn't deserve her anger, or her fear, or whatever it was she was feeling. But she couldn't seem to stop herself.

"Nik, that wasn't—"

"Fair? You know what's not fair, Becky? Is you trying to steal my son."

"We didn't—"

"Do you have any idea how worried I was when I realized he was gone?" Becky opened her mouth to say something, but before she could, Nikki delivered the blow she knew would hurt the most. "Of course you don't," she spat. "You don't have any children of your own. There's no way you could possibly know how it feels."

She knew the words would hurt. And in all her life, Nikki had never said anything so cruel, especially not to her best friend. The second the words were out of her mouth and Becky recoiled, seeming to collapse on herself, she wanted to take them back. But it was too late. Becky turned and ran, dumping the cups of hot chocolate in a nearby garbage can as she made her escape.

Nikki was rooted to the spot, unable to move. Her chest heaved and she struggled to catch her breath. It took a moment for her to look around. People were staring, and she hadn't even realized she'd raised her voice. But of course people were watching them. Nikki and her illegitimate child must be the talk of the town. Her eyes floated across the crowd, not registering on any one face until they landed on Matt.

She couldn't quite make out his expression, but by the way his mouth was set in a firm line and his arm wrapped around Ryan, pulling him close, she could guess what he was thinking. She had to get out of there. She couldn't just stand in the middle of the town square, acting as the entertainment for everyone. But, still, she couldn't move.

An arm clamped down on her shoulder, and a gentle voice said, "Nikki. Come with me."

She nodded numbly and let the owner of the voice lead her away. The crowd parted for them as they walked and Nikki was glad for the strong arm that held on to her, because she didn't trust her legs to hold her up. It wasn't until she was sitting in a chair behind one of the many craft huts that lined the square, and a foam cup of coffee was put in her hands, that she bothered to look at her savior.

Santa Claus.

Of course. She recognized the voice on some level.

"Thank you, Levi," she said.

"Just drink that and calm yourself down," he said, gruffly. "You're not going to be any good until you get a hold of your emotions."

Nikki almost smiled at the older man as he shook his head and muttered something about women and their moods. He looked almost comical, pacing in his big red suit in front of her.

"Ryan? I should—"

"He's with Matt," Levi said. He pulled up a chair and sat across from her. "I think it's best if he stays there for a bit longer, don't you?"

She nodded, and then a thought hit her. "Oh no. Did he see me…I can't believe…what does—"

"It's okay, Nikki. I don't know how much he saw, but he's a smart kid, that boy. He knows something's up and sometimes it's good for a child to see their mama be human. He'll be okay."

She shook her head and inhaled the hot coffee, using the moment to calm down. "I'm sorry," she said after a moment. "I shouldn't have said any of that. I didn't really mean it."

"I'm sure you didn't," Levi said. "But it's not me who needs apologizing to. And I think you know that."

"I do," she whispered. "I just want what's best for Ryan." Nikki looked up into Levi's kind eyes. "I just wish I knew what that was."

"I think you know." He patted her leg. "You're a good mama, Nikki. And sometimes being a good mama means making the tough decisions."

She smiled weakly. "How do you know all this?"

Levi's smile grew sad and his voice dropped when he said, "For more than fifteen years after your dad passed, I watched your mama do right by you. She was something."

"Yes she was." Nikki's eyes filled with tears again. "I wish she was here now. She'd know what to do."

They sat in silence for a moment, each of them lost in their own thoughts, while Nikki sipped at her coffee. It was Levi who broke the silence. "What do you think she would have said, Nikki?"

Nikki didn't hesitate when she answered. "She would have told me to stay." A tear slid down her cheek and she didn't bother to wipe it away before another fell. "She never said, but that's all she ever wanted."

Levi nodded. The old man's own eyes glistened with unshed tears.

Nikki knew what she wanted. And she knew what was right. "I think," she said, "maybe I could stay. At least for a little while," she added quickly. "I owe it to Matt and Ryan. They need to get to know each other. And, after everything she did for me, I owe it to my mom, too."

A sob overtook her, and Nikki gave herself over to the tears she'd been holding in for too long.

Levi's warm, safe arms wrapped around her and held her while she cried. "And you, Nikki," he whispered gruffly in her ear. "You owe this to yourself, too."

###

AFTER HER TEARS WERE SPENT, Nikki pulled herself together and set out to find Matt and Ryan. But first, she had an apology to make and it was long overdue. It didn't take long to find Becky. Nikki knew her old friend well, and she hadn't changed that much in ten years.

Just as she'd guessed, Becky was standing at the bake sale table, taking in the goodies and fresh baked treats for sale. Ever since they were kids, Becky'd always used chocolate to feel better. And from what she understood, it had served her well in life with her successful baking blog. Becky didn't know it, but ever since her mom told her about it, Nikki had become one of Becky's most faithful followers.

She took a deep breath before she approached her. People were watching, but she didn't care. Nothing else mattered except making right what she'd broken so many years ago.

"Becky?"

Her friend stiffened, and turned slowly. Her eyes were red and her make-up smudged, but she was still the same beautiful Becky.

"Can we talk?" Nikki asked.

Becky nodded and in a vain effort to give them some privacy, Nikki led them to a small bench. "I'm sorry," she said without waiting. "I was totally out of line and I need you to know that I didn't mean any of that. I just—"

"You're scared."

Nikki let out a long breath. "Yes," she said. "I'm terrified."

"I know this is hard." Becky's lips turned up in a small smile. She took Nikki's hand. "Heck, it's hard for all of us. But you don't have to be scared, Nik. We're family."

It took her a minute to process what Becky was saying.

"And we don't want to take Ryan away from you," Becky continued. "We would never do that."

Nikki nodded.

"But we do want to know him and be part of his life."

"Of course." Nikki thought of earlier when she'd seen Matt and Ryan laughing together. "I want that, too," she said, and meant it.

Becky's smile got bigger and she said, "Should we go find the —Matt and Ryan?" She caught herself, no doubt remembering the way Nikki had flown off the handle the last time she referred to them so casually.

Nikki nodded. "But first..." She pulled Becky into a hug and held her old friend tightly. "I'm so, so sorry, Becky," she said without releasing her. "I never wanted to hurt you and—"

"It's okay."

"No. It's not. I can't change it. Any of it. But I need you to know that, okay?"

Becky nodded and pulled away. There were tears shining in her eyes. "I know it, Nik. I do. And you're right, we can't change it. So, what do you say we move forward, together?"

"I'd like that." Nikki's own eyes filled up again. "Damn tears," she said with a laugh. "Come on, let's go find the boys."

EPILOGUE

~Nikki~

BAGS IN HAND, Nikki stepped out of the Evergreen Grocer and onto the sidewalk. She inhaled deeply, letting her lungs fill with the fresh spring air. She'd always loved this time of year in Halfway, when the snow was melting, the trees were budding, and everything was slowly starting to come to life again. She took her time walking down the sidewalk, letting her mind drift. When she reached her car, she dropped her groceries off before continuing down the street to her next destination.

What was meant to be a few days in Halfway turned into a few weeks. And finally, it just made sense to enroll Ryan in classes. The longer they spent in town, the more they both felt as if they were home. Not to mention the way Ryan and Matt were together. At first there'd been a bit of awkwardness between them as they tried to figure out their roles with each other. But Nikki couldn't believe how quickly even that vanished as they easily slipped into a comfortable father-son relationship. It made Nikki's heart happy to see them together. And with each day that passed, she knew she would never take it away from them.

The bells over the door tinkled as she walked into the flower shop. She couldn't hide the smile when Parker called from the back of the shop. "I'll be right there," he said.

Nikki didn't say anything as she picked out a small bouquet of yellow roses and went to the counter to wait for him.

"Sorry," Parker said as he came out of the back room. "I was just finish—Nikki?" His handsome face split into a grin at the sight of her. "What are you doing here?"

She held up the bouquet. "It's my mom's birthday today. Yellow roses were her favorite."

Parker's smile fell. "I'm sorry," he said and moved around the corner to pull her into his arms.

"It's okay," she said when he released her. "Honestly. I'm fine." And she was. For the first time in a long time, Nikki felt good about things and even though there was an ache in her heart every time she thought of her mother, it was okay. "I just wanted to get her some flowers," she said. "It felt right."

"Of course." Parker took another look at her, likely making sure she really was okay and wasn't going to melt down into a puddle of tears, before heading around to the other side of the counter. "But there's no charge." He took the flowers and wrapped them up. "Not for Marie."

Nikki smiled gratefully and took the bouquet. "Thank you," she whispered.

He shrugged and the smile appeared on his face again. "But we're still on for later, right?"

"Absolutely." Nikki straightened up and tossed her hair behind her shoulder in an effort to flirt. "I can't wait to cook you my specialty. Chicken parmesan." She didn't point out that it wasn't really her specialty. In fact, she'd never actually cooked it before, but she really wanted their date to be special.

They'd been seeing each other for a few months, but with their busy schedules and Ryan of course, they couldn't seem to find much time to be alone. But that was all about to change. With Ryan staying over at Matt and Becky's, Nikki was determined to make their first night alone together as special as possible.

"You know, we can go out." Parker looked down at the counter, wiping some unseen smudge off the glass. "I heard the Spruce Grill has a new pasta dish that's supposed to be really good."

"Parker, I—"

"If you don't want pasta, their steak sandwich is—"

"Parker," she said with more force behind her voice. "I'm going to cook. I want to. I already bought the groceries."

"Okay," he said, his voice laced with doubt. "If you really want to. But I'm bringing dessert, so we have something to eat." He added the last part with a mumble under his breath.

"Hey." She put her hands on her hips. "I don't know what you think you know about my cooking. But I'll have you know that I'm pretty good in the kitchen."

"That's not the way I remember it."

She stopped to think for a minute about what he could possibly be talking about. When the realization hit her, she burst into laughter. "Wait," she said, trying to gulp back her giggle. "Are you talking about the chili I made in senior year?"

He nodded, looking at her with worry.

"Parker. That was ten years ago. I'm a much better cook than that now. I was just a kid."

"A guy doesn't get over that many chili peppers." His voice was completely serious, but his face split into a smile. "But you're right, that was a long time ago," he said.

Parker's words were heavy with meaning, and Nikki nodded. "Yes. It was. And a lot can change in ten years."

As if to prove her point, she leaned across the counter and

took his face into her hands, placing a soft, sweet kiss directly on his lips.

"I'll see you later." With a small wave, she took the flowers and left the shop. She had two more stops to make before she could head home and start cooking for her date.

It was a short drive to the Jennings' farm, and Nikki hopped out of the car without hesitation. Becky would be waiting for her, and she didn't have much time. She didn't bother knocking as she opened the door and called, "Hey. I'm here."

"In the kitchen."

Nikki smiled. *As if Becky would be anywhere else.*

Her friend was behind the counter, covered in flour, with a big smile on her face and a mouthwatering smell coming from the oven. "What are you baking? It smells amazing."

"Ryan's favorite. A triple chocolate fudge cake," she said. "Here, try this." She held out a bowl and Nikki stuck her finger in the icing. Her eyes closed and she let out a small groan of pleasure.

"No wonder that's Ryan's favorite. It's seriously the most delicious thing ever. Way better than the ones I used to pick up from the grocery store."

"Oh no." Becky looked horrified. "You did not feed that poor boy grocery store cakes. No wonder he's insatiable for my baking."

Nikki laughed. "The kitchen has always been your strong suit," she said. "Not mine." She looked around. "Where are the boys?"

"Matt's got them out checking the fields," Becky said. "I think they're mostly looking to see if the streams are all thawed. But they won't admit that. When they found out Ryan had never been fishing before, Levi got it in his head that they need to fix that problem as soon as possible."

A flush of shame crossed Nikki's face. Of course Ryan would like to go fishing. She'd never thought that he might be missing out on that by not having a father in his life. But now that he had a father in Matt and an unexpected grandfather figure in Levi, there was no doubt they'd catch him up on everything he'd missed.

"Stop that," Becky said, waving her towel in Nikki's direction. "There's nothing to be upset about. Here, have some more icing." Becky thrust the bowl at her again, and Nikki happily took a large finger full.

"Yummy. You seriously have to teach me to make that."

"One thing at a time." Becky laughed and wiped her hands on her apron. She reached for her giant binder that Nikki knew was her cookbook and dropped it on the counter between them. "Here's the recipe." She opened the rings and carefully withdrew the page. "It's super easy to follow and you shouldn't be able to screw it up."

Nikki raised her eyebrow.

"I said, you *shouldn't* but you have to follow the directions. Did you get all the ingredients I told you to?"

Nikki nodded.

"Good. Then you'll be fine."

"I hope so," Nikki said, taking the paper. "It's kind of an important dinner."

"Is it?" Becky wiggled her eyebrows and Nikki swatted at her. "Well, it's about time," Becky said. "Parker's great. You know I want you to be happy."

"I know."

"It's all I've ever wanted, Nik."

They locked eyes across the counter and it was Nikki who reached out and squeezed her friend's hand. "I know," she said. "And I am. I really am."

"So am I. You have no idea how much it means to me that you're—"

"Me too." Nikki cut her off, not needing her to finish the sentence. "I'm glad I'm here, too."

They stared at each other for another minute before Becky broke the serious moment. "Okay. That's enough of this blubbering. You have a big night ahead of you, so look over the recipe and make sure you know what to do. Chicken parmesan isn't hard. But if someone's going to screw it up, it's going to be you. I love you, Nik, but…"

"I know, I know."

After a few more instructions from Becky, Nikki was on her way with only one more stop to make before she went home to start preparing for her date. She glanced over at the bouquet of roses that sat on her front seat. *Yes*, she thought. *One more very important stop.*

The graveyard was quiet as Nikki made her way through the still brown grass, to the spot where they'd buried her mother, right where she wanted to be: under a large spruce tree, next to Nikki's father, who'd died when Nikki herself was just three years old.

She knelt on the ground, still cold from the thaw, and laid the flowers down. "Happy birthday, Mom. I know it's not much of a celebration this year, but I wanted you to know I didn't forget. I know you'd probably want a big party, but I don't think any of us are ready for that this year." She smiled a little. "We still miss you too much. But I brought you your favorite flowers, and I did get you a present."

Nikki hugged her knees close and looked up to the sky, taking her time. "I know you already know what it is," she said. "But I wanted to make sure you know that we're here, in Halfway. Ryan and me. And you know what, Mom? We're happy. We should have come years ago, but…it wasn't time. I guess in a weird way, I have you to thank for bringing me back."

The idea that her mother's death was the catalyst for her happiness wasn't a new one. But Nikki couldn't let herself feel guilty, and she knew her mother wouldn't have wanted it. All her mother ever wanted was for her to come home and be happy. It wouldn't have mattered to her how it happened.

"I'm home, Mom," Nikki whispered to the sky. "I'm finally home."

~**Want to know more**? **Find out what happens during the next festival in Halfway...Turn the page...**~

DISCOVER THE HALFWAY SERIES

HALFWAY TO NOWHERE

Book 1

DISCOVER THE HALFWAY SERIES

HALFWAY IN BETWEEN

Book 2

DISCOVER THE HALFWAY SERIES

HALFWAY TO CHRISTMAS

Book 3

ABOUT ELENA AITKEN

Elena Aitken is a USA Today Bestselling Author of more than fifty romance and women's fiction novels. The mother of 'grown up' twins, Elena now lives with her very own mountain man in the heart of the very mountains she writes about. She can often be found with her toes in the lake and a glass of wine in her hand, dreaming up her next book and working on her own happily ever after.

Subscribe to Elena's Newsletter and never miss a thing!

THE SPRINGS
CASTLE MOUNTAIN LODGE

Let's Connect
www.elenaaitken.com
Elena@elenaaitken.com

ABOUT STEENA HOLMES

Steena Holmes is a NYT and USA Today Bestselling Author with almost 3 million books sold worldwide. She writes Women's Fiction, Contemporary Fiction and Psychological Thrillers & Suspense. Listed as one of the top 20 women to read by Good Housekeeping, there's bound to be a story you won't soon forget in her catalog.

Join Steena's mailing list and grab a free read - and if you're a fellow travel lover like her, come join one of her upcoming reader trips!

www.steenaholmes.com
steena@steenaholmes.com

Made in United States
North Haven, CT
11 March 2024